WHERE THE LIGHT
FLICKERS

WHERE THE LIGHT FLICKERS

RYAN BURDEN

ISBNs: 979-8-9990422-5-5 (paperback); 979-8-9990422-4-8 (ebook)

Library of Congress Control Number: 2025944808

First Printing: 2025

Printed in the United States of America

Praise for Ryan Burden

Ryan Burden writes with a dazzling combination of stoic restraint, profound insight, and poignant lyricism. This is big-hearted, undaunted, and epic storytelling miraculously broken into small, intimate canvases, all emblazoned with some of the finest sentences I've ever seen from a debut novelist. *Where the Light Flickers* is a meditative, spellbinding work about the complicated and often impossible moral dilemmas facing those struggling to survive in a marginalized, forgotten place.

— Dean Bakopoulos, author of *Please Don't Come Back From the Moon*

A book of messy lives immaculately told, *Where the Light Flickers* is lyric, wise, and, not least, thrilling. Ryan Burden is a masterful craftsman and this debut is the exquisite result.

— Liam Callanan, author of *When in Rome* and *Paris by the Book*

This book is dedicated to the many patient teachers who have helped it on its way, and to T., who inspired its beginning. To my loving, even more patient family: the next one's for you.

"Man is the only creature who refuses to be what he is."

— ALBERT CAMUS

CHAPTER 1

SHOKTEN

It's not long since the short day ended, slipping almost instantly from twilight into dark, the way it always does in this valley, which is bordered to the north and south by hills and, to the west, by mountains. Now the only light comes from the windows of scattered houses and the lazy flicker of fireflies floating peacefully above their lawns.

The dog—a ropey ridgeback mutt—has come a long way from his home up in the mountains, looking for a place to die. He's been traveling since early afternoon, first sliding down beds of shale left by the mining company's extractions, then weaving through the blasted creek-bed between the empty shells of abandoned trailer homes. Pain pulses between his legs and he knows he doesn't have much time to find shelter. The path is rough, but he won't stop out in the open. Instinct tells him to hide.

If he could question it, he might decide this instinct is more than caution. That it's more about finding a quiet place to think before the very end. Maybe, deep down, he would find something poetic in the way we enter this world in a crowd, but always leave it alone. Maybe these thoughts would thicken, calcifying into tales that he might tell himself, about why the pain feels sharper in the cool air, or why the smell of woodsmoke reminds him of something he never quite lived. About the shape of his shadow on the barn wall, bent and trembling. Maybe he'd imagine he's not dying.

Whatever tales he might tell, they wouldn't help. They wouldn't offer any comfort. They would only vex. And so, it's just as well that he cannot tell tales at all.

CHAPTER 2

VALLEY

In the kitchen of a house down in the valley, Hem is arguing with his daughter Kate. He stands stiffly by the propane stove while she sits opposite him on the stairs, one hand resting on the rail. They've been arguing for a while, and every sentence now is just a louder version of the first.

He's upset because she says she's going to marry Connor Biel, a miner from Mania, ten miles up the coast. Though he doesn't say it, he believes if he had more time—to argue, to steady his thoughts—he might find the words to stop her. He imagines something convincing: a logical takedown she couldn't ignore, or a heartfelt speech. But all he can manage are pleas. Again, he asks her to delay the wedding.

"You're the one who moved us out of Providence," she says. "You can't say no one here is good enough."

Hem turns to put the kettle on, convinced that things might calm down if they can just share some tea. He's embarrassed that she has managed to stay calm, while he has many times forgotten himself and let his voice rise.

Still, when he shuts his eyes to think of something new to say, he doesn't see the calm, close-fitting darkness of his own mind, but the vast dark he imagines must be at the very bottom of the Federal Mine. He sees her lips against the neck of a pale young miner, his calloused fingers intertwined with hers; his greasy hands gripping her waist. It's too dark to tell whose breath or movement is whose.

"I never said no one was good enough. I just thought you'd go to school back home."

The word hangs there—home—pressing down on all the fragile threads between them. Hem can't remember when he last called Providence home. Back when they moved, he was afraid to let the others think about going back. He wanted them to get used to the valley, even though he knew he couldn't. It's taken seven years and this news to convince him that they never will.

Kate says, "I've talked to Connor. He says he'll help me pay for school."

"You mean because I can't?"

"Of course, because you can't."

Now, Hem stares out the window at the silver shadow of the creek.

"You could have tried for a scholarship."

"And you know I'm not smart enough."

Hem shrugs. "But smart enough to wait to tell your father that you're marrying some guy from Mania he's never met."

She hugs herself beneath his glare. "It's not like I knew all that long ago. It happened fast."

"I gather."

On the lawn, Lorraine and Trevor are out stalking fireflies. Lorraine is small and slender, just like Kate, and Trevor has grown tall recently, so Hem has some trouble telling them apart. Lately, he has concluded that his family has reached a turning point—a great divide at which they would prefer to leave him and continue traveling alone. He can't pinpoint why, but suspects each has their own reason. He has no talent for considering more than one thought at a time. His mind narrows like a choke.

"I've seen that kid. Sitting around the old factory with the others. You think I don't notice."

"It doesn't mean he's doing anything wrong."

"Well, it sure as hell doesn't look right."

"Maybe I'll go to veterinary school. That way, I can be exactly like you."

"Don't pretend the problem's money. You're stuck here because you never wanted education in the first place."

The tea leaves swell and curl as Hem covers them with water. As they both fall into quiet, he can feel his anger fade into exhaustion. When he sets her cup in front of her, she stares at it intensely, shielding her thoughts.

Though he's only nine, Lorraine worries that Trevor is already turning out like his father. Tonight, he was the first to see the fireflies out on the lawn, and he already had his boots on and a jar in his hand long before she had a chance to think about dissuading him. He thinks too much like Hem, which will undoubtedly lead him to a job like Hem's, and caring more about it than the people all around him.

Normally, she'd have sent him with Hem or let him go alone, but she promised she wouldn't be there when Kate told Hem about the wedding. So, instead, she finds herself here, ankle-deep in mud beside the creek, arms stretched towards a firefly that Trevor has decided he must catch. It's a little bigger than the ten or twelve he has already trapped inside his jar, but otherwise no different. She guesses that he has another experiment planned—like the model rockets he's been building all winter.

Lorraine hasn't caught fireflies since she was a kid, but her hands still remember the feel of them fluttering and the quiet satisfaction when they calm. One crawls along her hand to her fingertip. She thinks about letting it go, but Trevor shouts,

"Got him!" and she can't bring herself to disappoint him. She slides the bug into his jar. It feels like a betrayal, though she isn't sure why.

"There," she says as he clamps the lid. "Do we have enough now?"

Trevor looks up at the sky, frowning, like the answer's hidden up there. Then he bends over and peers into the jar.

"They aren't bright enough yet. I want them to blink all at once."

It's been about an hour since they left the house, so Kate and Hem are likely still arguing. Lorraine doesn't think marrying Connor is the right move, but maybe it's Kate's best chance. Their savings are gone, used up in court. Kate will have to find her own way. What meager savings she and Hem had scraped together are long gone, spent on legal counsel for the suit. She knows that Kate will have to carve her own place in the world, and she knows that after all the arguing and bickering is done, her husband will be forced to recognize this, too.

"We need more," Trevor says.

She tries not to stumble as she sits to dry her feet beside the stream.

"It won't help. There aren't enough. They'll suffocate each other."

Trevor studies the jar, thinking hard—the exact way she wishes he wouldn't.

He asks how long the fireflies will live in his room if he sets them free.

"Not long. You'll wake up with a bunch of dead bugs in your bed."

He winces, tucks the jar under his arm, and marches off.

Lorraine turns towards the house. Through the window, she sees Hem watching her, lost in one of his daydreams. Her feet are cold and shriveled. She rolls her socks over them and stuffs them into her boots.

"Where are you going?" she calls.

"To try it in the barn!"

Somewhere nearby, an engine hums. She looks up towards the flat-topped mountains, thinking it might be a plane, but it's too dark to see. What she sees instead is just her mind's projection on the sky's black screen.

Hem often sees young men like Connor Biel when he goes into Shokten. They are invariably dirty and disheveled, humping through the town like zombies as they make their way out to the bars after a long shift at the mine.

This early in the evening, they look worn out, but by nightfall, they'll turn wild, stumbling drunk through the streets. He's never done the work they do, but he can imagine it—knees aching, lungs and liver damaged, eyes losing their shine. He doesn't want that for Kate. He doesn't think she should even have to know that kind of life exists, let alone live near it.

They've been silent for a long time now, both staring moodily into their tea.

Hem says, "You think that he can give you things. I don't know what—"

"—it doesn't matter—"

"—but he will never give you anything, you see? He won't have any left."

Kate reaches back and pulls her hair into a tight ponytail so her forehead shines. "I'm tired. You're not making any sense."

If he were honest, Hem might say that he regrets forcing them out into this valley. He might say that if he had money, he would send her back to Providence. If he were honest, Kate might tell him that she's just afraid of leaving home, and thinks it will be better if she's not alone.

Instead, they simply stare at one another. Hem thinks about how little Kate looks like her mother. Kate thinks of how old her father has become in just the few years since the move. She tries and finds she can't imagine Connor with the same stooped shoulders and sunken chest, same yellowed eyes and rough, gray skin.

She thinks he's too strong to succumb to these afflictions and will age with all the grace of a great actor.

"Kate—" Hem says, "I can't tell you—"

They hear shouting from the yard. Both turn in unison and soon hear Trevor's footsteps pounding up the path between the house and the barn.

"Dad! I found a dog!"

Hem sets down his cup. "Kate—"

"I've got it," she says, already handing him the flashlight.

THEY ALL FOLLOW Lorraine down the dirt path into the night. She walks ahead of them, pale in her faded jeans and undershirt.

She catches Trevor by the arm as he tries to dart past her towards the barn.

"Stay with me," she says. "You don't want to get bit."

The air is filled with insects and the smell of spruce; the bitter tastes of onion grass and clover. Hem wonders if Lorraine already knows about the wedding. Probably—he's always been the last to find out. He tries to calm himself by counting stones along the path as they're illuminated by the long beam of his light.

At the barn, he waves the others back and goes inside alone, moving slowly, sweeping the light ahead. He finds more stones, some limp straw, and a haze of dust. Though he can't see the dog, he knows it's young and male. He smells it even through the reek of gasoline and wood.

"Dad?" says Trevor.

"What."

"Don't hurt him."

"What?"

"He's hurt already. Just don't hurt him anymore."

"Stay quiet," says Lorraine, "and let your father work."

Finally, he finds the dog all curled up behind a fertilizer bag. He whispers for Kate to get his bag. He thinks he might try a tranquilizer, but isn't sure how bad the injury is. He inches forward, one hand held out in a fist. The dog growls. Then it starts to whimper.

The barn is full of insect hum and the soft meowing of cats in the loft. Hem's light shines on its hind legs, which both lie limply in a pool of blood. The way it's holding itself, he thinks he knows what happened. In his mind, he sees the dog splayed out and cowering, then screaming as it feels the first prick of the knife. He sees it squirming, biting, and running headlong through a backyard littered with debris, careening, bleeding frantic patterns in the dirt.

"Here," Kate says. She has his bag along with a clean towel, which she's folded neatly in a square. "How bad is he?"

Hem shuts his eyes. "I don't know, but he's bleeding like he's cut an artery."

"Can you fix it?"

He gives her the flashlight and slowly lifts the dog's leg. Underneath it is a mess of blood and swollen skin.

The dog starts to shiver and growl again.

"You're okay, Sonny," Hem says. "You're okay."

"What is it?"

He stuffs the towel against the wound. "It looks like someone tried to castrate him."

The dog's eyes are a vacillating shade of green. They cloud and clear, and when they clear, he sees an image of himself reflected in them.

Kate kneels and opens up his bag. She once used to play

his assistant. Now, the motions are familiar; she completes them without thinking.

Hem says, "Stop. Not in here. We'll just infect him."

"Oh," Kate says. "I thought—"

He shines the light into the bag and sees the bottle she's holding. It is large, much bigger than her hand—the last of his expired stash of pentobarbital.

Back in Providence, when he still held a license, this had been his drug of choice. Of course, he knew that Kate was old enough to notice all the animals that came in kennels through the front door and then left in trash bags through the back, but he did not know she had paid such close attention.

Now, they share a look of understanding. In a way, Hem thinks he's proud of her. He thinks that she might see the world with much clearer eyes than he imagined.

He takes the bottle from her hand and drops it back into the bag.

He says, "You'll have to help me lift him."

This is when it starts, when Hem decides that he will not let this dog die.

CHAPTER 3

MOUNTAIN

All that he remembers, for as long as he remembers, is the mountain.

Mason is a child, but he's old enough to recognize the limitations of the world as it's offered to him. He's left the mountain more than once—has been to the surrounding towns: the park and library in Cavalcade, the old amusement park in Mania, and even the shops in Providence, the major city inland. Almost every day, he boards a bus that takes him down into the valley to the small school in Shokten, where he's a student in fifth grade. But he doesn't think he'll ever see much farther, so he's instead contrived to travel inward, building up around him an impenetrable shell of daydreams and silence.

The mountain is a squat and spreading pile, melting down into the valley like a mound of mud. Its top is flattened, blasted off, and scoured out by men in search of coal. The bus will trundle over this uncovered ground, the morning sunlight coming from below to paint the ceiling with its pale gold glow, then suddenly shift down and drop onto the road that leads into the valley.

Mason is unlike the other children, who take time to greet their homes. He never spares a thought for his inviting room, or for his rock collection, or his tattered books of science fiction. Instead, he screws his eyes up tight and tries to conjure answers to all the inevitable dinner table questions.

How was school?

The same.

Was lunch all right?

A shrug.

He always eats his lunch but makes sure he complains about it now and then, asking if he can have ham instead of pepperoni or for ketchup mixed into his mayonnaise. He doesn't know if he likes his home because he has never known anything else. This is how his father tells it: In the beginning, there was only a peninsula, with steep mountains through its middle and cold, rocky beaches all around. Mason's great-great-grandfather, Edmund, used it as an escape from Providence, besides its being a good place to make untaxed whiskey. There were other men who eventually followed him. And women, too. Edmund had Kurt, Mason's great-grandfather, and Kurt had Rig, who had Mason's father, Spoon.

It is a strange thing to be famous in a small town. Everyone pays attention to you, whether they are trying to or not. They hear his name is Sullivan and quickly change, either making some excuse to leave or acting overly nice, as though they admired him just for being who he is. Only Trevor ever treated him like a normal kid, and Mason thinks it's because he (somehow) doesn't know.

In any case, he has spent all day, as he does every day, preparing for this moment—when his bedroom door is closed, and the lights are turned off so that he's sitting in a tumbling aquarium of blues and blacks, with aspen shadows flickering at his feet. He takes his time getting into bed—adjusting the sheets and blankets so they all align, punching up his thin pillow, and finally burrowing down into the mattress like a vole.

He hears the mountain calling him outside his window. It has a name for him—a name it whispers on a breath that smells of blasted earth and granite. It's not a name he can pronounce, but he knows by the sound of it that it is his and that it is an insult.

As he takes his seat for dinner, Mason's father asks him if he knows a boy named Fisher. Mason says he doesn't think he does. His father answers through a mouthful of baked beans.

"Family took off somewhere. No one seems to know."

His mother has her eyes closed and has not touched food since they sat down.

"They're gone for good, Spoon," she says. "Everybody knows it."

Mason's father rolls his eyes. "Don't worry, I'm not going too far after anybody for a thousand dollars."

Now he winks at Mason, grabs the pan of beans, and pushes it across the table.

Mason says, "I've had enough."

Spoon cocks his head and stares at him with narrowed eyes. It is a look that Mason hates. It makes him feel as though his father is deliberately searching for an explanation—not from Mason's mouth, but in the private space between the front of his skull and its back.

"I'm not hungry," Mason says again.

"Well, if you're finished, you can go and feed the dogs."

"Gone forever," Mason's mother says. Her head drifts softly backward, like a balloon. "Nobody ever sees those Fishers. Not ever again."

It is a walk of seventy steps from the kitchen door out to the kennel. Mason counts them quickly, each soft footfall in the blue dust, each sharp snap of a twig. The darkness closets him and seems to bear him along with it, like a passenger in its velvety car. It takes him gently down the path to the kennel door, where it finally pauses. He can hear the sounds of restless dogs in motion all along the walls. As he stands listening, he hears one risk a plaintive whine. This is the third night he has heard such whining since a week ago when he stopped giving them their food.

Mason is of two minds. He would like the dogs to die, but he did not think it would take this long. He thought that they would simply quiet down and, in a few days, slip away mysteriously, as if caught by some unknown disease. Now he thinks that he will have to feed them soon before their father notices and checks the level of food left in the bin. But he won't feed them tonight. Instead, he covers up his ears and walks on past the kennel to the place where the flat mountain's summit starts its steep decline into the valley. Here, he stops to look up at the stars. He knows the names of every one of them, whether he has found them in his books or made them up himself. They are familiar to him, comforting in their slow revolutions, so unlike the antic house lights in the valley, which he fears he will never be able to explain.

His grandfather once told him that a person's soul is brought to him by doves and carried off by owls. He said that he once knew a woman who could send a pigeon flying and see everything that it saw with her own eyes. He said some people have this gift. Mason is too old to believe that it will work, but too young not to try.

He has set a trap, baited with a crust of bread, in the long grass near the mountain's edge. Tonight, he finds the bread has turned to plaster and is quickly crumbling and blowing off its hook. He knocks it all away and takes a new piece from his pocket, wrapped up neatly in a sheet of notebook paper. He hopes to catch a bird soon, which he will release from the window of the bus just as it makes the turn around the boulder at the end of the drive. He will point his eyes and his mind at it as it flies away from him, and he will follow it and make his long-anticipated escape.

There are just a few more minutes left before his father will expect him home. Mason sits cross-legged at the edge of the cliff, watching all the momentary flickers in the lights that shine from every window in the town below. He knows that each one means a body passing and has made a game of trying to decide what they may be. Tonight, he counts six people, a horse, and a cloud of fireflies out of a thousand other indistinguishable shifts.

The compass of a universe does not depend on fact, but on the limited experiences of the minds inhabiting it. This is proven best in small towns which have been small all their lives —especially in isolated places, where the normal contact with the wider world is a garbled line, one carrying a slew of signals drifting from definitive commands to whispered static— where the rule of primal and uneducated nature still, at times, appears sound.

CHAPTER 4

CHURCH

Every Monday, Spoon attends the local concert at the small church in Shokten. He arrives half an hour early, just before the old men wander in like pilgrims with their stained guitars, their gut-string banjos, and their tarnished harps.

He feels comfortable around these people, but he likes to think that he's from a different stock. The Sullivans have always lived with both eyes keen on personal advantage, and Spoon's mind is cold and calculating as an abacus. He's a merchant in the purest sense, with an abiding love not only for the money that things represent but for the things themselves and for the process of attaining them. He has some admiration for the instruments these men hold so compassionately as he does for the instinctive skill with which they play them. But he doesn't understand why these men, who spend their entire work week sweating in the mine, insist on wasting every weekend entertaining others. He can only guess that they have not been blessed with the intelligence to live their lives in any other way and pities them for their misfortune.

When he goes to listen to the concerts, Spoon is always

drunk. He likes to think he has inherited this habit from his ancestors, who took it up for courage and never learned how to stop. He starts his drinking at Fitzpatrick's Lanes, along with all the other men whom he employs or who do not have anywhere more reasonable to go. On every other day, he drinks in his own bar, far out of town, and when he drinks in company, he doesn't like to do so anywhere else. He comes into town on Mondays just because it's closer to the church, and he doesn't like driving too far when he's drunk.

Today, his hours at the Lanes have left him in a dusky mood. Today, he drank with March. They drank back in Spoon's private room, where they could talk about the recent death of March's wife. All morning, Spoon deferred while March talked in infuriating circles about Cathleen, and about Tommy Fitzpatrick, with whom she had slept the night before she died, and then about his rambling old house, which he worried was becoming structurally unsound.

Spoon thinks March is going soft. He drinks too much lately, and he sits on his stool like a wet flour sack, breathing fast and heavy in between his frequent coughs.

Today, Spoon left the Lanes an hour early to drink alone in his truck while he waited for the pastor to arrive and open up the church. They did not look at one another as the pastor opened the door. The Sullivans are never welcome at the Sunday service, as the people in town know their business and do not explicitly approve. They all believe in a divided world—clean and unclean—body and soul. Spoon is well aware that they expect him to play a scapegoat for their sins. He knows but hardly ever thinks about it. He does not, in any case, think much about what he does or doesn't believe. He comes to these small concerts for the same reason his father did: because he doesn't want to seem to hold himself aloof. But he has found that he enjoys the music, especially the songs about death, which he finds soothing in their repetition, their plodding refrains, each note confidently honest. When he hears these songs, he often thinks about his father, who died young. The whole peninsula was different, then, before the mine and so before the towns that sprang up all around it, bringing with them a disturbing love for law and order. Rig Sullivan was too proud to lie low. He heard the state police were coming for him, and he turned his pistol on himself.

Spoon sits way up on the balcony, his feet up on the rail. He holds a folded bulletin in his left hand and strikes it hard against his knee on every offbeat. Men and women fill the front pews down below, all sourly content in their flowered dresses and their threadbare Oxford shirts. The men on stage kick off a waltz. A girl Spoon doesn't know stands out in the aisle, slowly tapping her feet from heel to toe and back again. At times, she reaches for her mother, sitting in the pew beside her, and they hold each other's hands and sway a little.

Spoon has always been uncommonly obsessed with certainty. He has a lust for the inevitable and romanticizes it the way that some men do the sea. His mind prefers hard men, the kind who would much rather misstep than deliberate too long, and he's constantly annoyed that such men are so difficult to find.

The final number is an upbeat mountain rag. Spoon rolls his head back in his pew and clicks his teeth. He cannot tear his mind from something March said: that a man can never know just how his life will go until the very end. Spoon stops his tapping, takes a moment to consider this, decides it is untrue, and pities March for having thought it.

Chapter 5

Mountain

It is early afternoon, and Spoon and Mason are both out. Fay is high again, and she has spent her morning trying unsuccessfully to make a cake. She doesn't know now if she meant it to be chocolate or vanilla, layer or pound, or even why she meant to make it in the first place. Stunned into a state of ecstasy, she caught up each of her ingredients, one at a time, and danced them up and down the hall between the kitchen and the den. She remembers the time when she and Spoon first danced together at the Lanes—the same day that she turned fifteen, and he began to pay her some attention. She remembers that dance as an ardent and sophisticated love affair. Today, she had a mind to replicate it perfectly, holding a pound bag of flour out at arm's length, cupping one egg in her palm to prove her movements elegant enough to keep from breaking it. Much later on, when she comes down, she will remember that first dance just as it was—both drunken and grotesque, a game she only played half-willingly because she did not feel Spoon's attitude allowed her to refuse. It's a re-enactment she will not recall. It will be blasted in her hurry to put all the food back in the kitchen, just where it belongs, before Spoon comes back home for dinner. He'll be angry if he sees her like this. He'll call her a junkie, which is painful when she knows it's true. But by that time, Fay will be fast asleep and fighting hard against the impulse to awaken.

There's nothing Fay hates more than coming down—the awful suffocation as the substance of reality regains its natural pressure. When, at times like this, she finds it unavoidable, she likes to stand with her face pressed against the kitchen window, staring out across the ridge at the interminable sky above the town. This lets her breathe more easily, though it's just a little more, and never more enough. Her view is partly checked by the sharp corner of the kennel, which she tries unsuccessfully to look past. In her agitation, she believes she sees the bricks begin to swell and wonders if this is because the days are growing warmer. She imagines the same swelling in the stones and boards throughout the house around her until soon she hears the creaking and sees the wall and window frame move slowly further away from her, pressed against her and threatening to collapse. And now the earth is swelling, too, a slow and even swelling like a rising loaf, accomplishing its distance purely, without crack or fissure. She's frightened by the thought that it might go on like this, constantly receding in every direction until she is left entirely alone on her small patch of faded gray linoleum.

She takes a sharp breath and turns from the window, running over to the sink, where she can turn the tap and watch the water rush out. With her head laid down against the sink's edge, she enjoys the simple sight of steady and unbroken flow. It is enough to make her absolutely tired of the choppy sea she feels her life has always been or has become, and she considers it just long enough to start thinking that she's part of it. She is a floundering fish caught up in the stream. She can't live without it.

As she stares at it, she feels her mind evaporate and pass

completely into it, then coalesce again and follow along with it, much like a dead man transported by his bearers. She's happy at first, rocking to the siren song of lost responsibility. But then the faucet groans and spurts, and she can feel a physical disruption in her chest and stomach, and she's angry and afraid to think she's so dependent. She must turn the water off. She knows this, so she does so slowly, choking out the stream by quarter-inch twists of the knob until there is a single drop left clinging to the spout. She turns away because she can't bear watching it fall.

Though her eyes are now closed, Fay knows the light has changed inside the kitchen. It has passed from solid into liquid, and now the sun has set. She knows when she decides to look that it will be the kind of light she often wishes she could drown herself in. But for now, she keeps her eyes shut while her racing mind spools down into a slow and abstract hum.

In her own darkness, Fay thinks of the things that she doesn't believe. For instance, she doesn't believe in violence. She doesn't believe in hate or in revenge. She doesn't think the world is a good place, an evil one, or one exactly in between. She thinks it is a place inhabited by ghosts, both good and evil, ghosts that live in everything and haunt the living every moment without end. There is the ghost of Spoon's belt coiled on the dresser and ghosts of Mason's rock collection strewn across his bedroom floor. Right now, she sees the awful, wasted ghost of her own mother in the faded needlepoint hung crookedly above the stove.

Fay does believe—and she believes unerringly—in all the ghosts that come to haunt her when she summons them by getting high. She doesn't blame Spoon's belt or Mason's rock collection for existing in their ghostly states—no more than she can blame the home and land around it for careening off into a distant shade of pale. The only thing that she resents is that these ghosts, which are all born of her own mind, have grown up selfish and care nothing for her in the end.

Fay opens up her eyes. The light is somewhat brighter than she had expected, but she won't shut her eyes again. She won't blink.

Spoon's raincoat hangs upon a crooked nail beside the door. His half-depleted whiskey bottle stands on the kitchen table. Far away from her, the sun is setting, and the moon is rising, making a pale halo on the ridge. The ghosts are strong now, creeping out from dusty corners and from cabinets. Fay hugs herself and wonders if, somehow, she has slept straight through fall and into winter.

Then the front door wobbles, screams, and she can feel again the warm air clinging to her skin.

CHAPTER 6

KATE

Kate said yes because she didn't think he meant it. She knows Connor is the kind of man who doesn't know himself and likely doesn't even want to. Sooner than most men do, he has reached a place where it seems smart to shed oneself, to drop the burden of self-consciousness and go on as an animal goes on, straight and honest and unchanging.

He took her by surprise. Later, when he told his friends and they began to welcome her as they had never done before —that is, as a true friend instead of as a passing fling—she felt for the first time certain of her future, which before then had been spread out like a shadow into which she had been constantly afraid of disappearing.

The grass at the edge of the path rustles, then stills. Kate lifts her eyes from the dark rim of her tea. A moment later, the porch groans.

"You out here?"

She doesn't answer. Connor steps into the square of light that spills from the kitchen window, his jacket slung over one shoulder, hands in his pockets. His boots scuff once on the step, then he sits beside her. The scents of oil and cedar cling to him.

"Your mom said you'd be outside."

Kate nods but doesn't look over.

They listen to the insects droning in the field.

"Hem still won't look at me," says Connor.

"Maybe he's trying not to make it real. Like bears. You know, if he doesn't move, maybe you'll go away."

"I make more noise than a bear."

"You smell like one."

He grins but doesn't push it. They lapse into silence again.

"He asked if I was gonna take you away," Connor says.

"And you said?"

"That depends. Are we escaping or eloping?"

Kate shrugs. "Either way, I'm not packing your socks." She tips the cup and drains what's left.

"Would you, though? Leave?"

"Where?"

"Somewhere quieter. Or louder. Just not here."

"Someplace with good sandwiches," he says. "I could work nights, you could do school. Or not. Could teach Sonny to bark at door-to-door evangelists."

The barn creaks again. Something small thuds.

"It's not about work," she says. "It's about starting."

"Starts are overrated."

"You think so?"

"Well, I started this conversation talking about your dad."

Kate laughs, the sound quick and breathy.

"Okay, so," he says, "What if we stayed? Got married." He pauses. "Maybe found you a better cup."

She eyes the chipped rim. "That does sound nice."

"See? Planning."

"Except then we wake up and you're your dad and I'm—"

"A world-renowned mug collector."

Kate grins. "Exactly."

A moth collides with the porch light. They both look.

"You scared?" she asks.

"Little. You?"

"Only of you getting sentimental."

"No risk there."

She leans against his shoulder. They sit that way a while, easy and unhurried.

Inside, the kettle begins to whistle. Neither of them moves.

CHAPTER 7

KENNEL

I t is just past noon—a hot day, though the air is bearable up on the mountain, where a stiff cross-breeze comes cutting over the peninsula from somewhere out at sea. Spoon is in his kennel, staring pointedly down at a bitch with a split nose, which he has found slugged up against the gate, curled tight despite the heat. Her breath comes shallow and a little loose. Her ribs are terribly distinct—the skin all puckered in between them. When he opens up the gate, she twitches one foot, rolls her eyes at him, and closes them again.

Her nose is half-pink, half-brown. Someone cut it down the middle, along the dividing line, so now it flares to both sides like a pig's. Spoon bought her for a hundred dollars from a breeder at the Providence dog auction one night after he had gotten drunk enough to think that she would make a profit. At the time, it had seemed simple—he'd call her a new breed, one raised by good, poor earthbound men—the kind of men who have to hunt to make a living and so take a survivalist's sound interest in their animals. He would explain to all the fat old men of the Hunt Club in Providence just how her flared nose helped her find the track. And he thought they would like that. He thought they would haggle and strike handshake deals and outmaneuver one another until Spoon went home with more than enough money for the dog he truly wanted—a pure-bred Pharaoh hound.

The next morning, feeling mean and guilty as he tapered off his drunk, he saw that he would never pass her off as anything but maimed. Still, she's some sort of hound, maybe a good one, and she interests him. Whoever cut her did it well. The wound has healed so smoothly that it almost looks natural.

Despite how frequently it happens, Spoon doesn't like seeing his dogs die.

He wonders if the bitch is well enough to eat and reaches for the bin. He lifts the lid, and when he does, all fifteen dogs inside the kennel rise. The sound they make is like a troop of soldiers who have just learned they are headed home.

Spoon sighs. He loves his dogs—he thinks of them as the complete, unfabricated evidence of his inherent talent to command. But he has been an idiot. He should have taken care of them himself.

He fills the bitch's bowl and sets it down in front of her. She growls a little—then she shivers to her feet and eats mechanically, as though she thinks that he will steal it back from her if given half a chance.

Spoon sighs again and lifts the food bin from its rack. He throws it, nipping off the lid and spilling a small avalanche of kibble out onto the floor. He walks down the aisle, opening the door of each cage as he goes. The dogs wait until he has passed to exit timidly and wander towards the food. At the end of the run, Spoon turns and watches them eat, thinking about two things. First, he thinks about what he will do to Mason when he gets home from school. Blurry images slip through his mind, flotsam churned up and pushed under by the mounting waves of his anger. Secondly, he thinks he's proud of how well he has trained his animals. Not one of them has made a sound.

CHAPTER 8

MOUNTAIN

Coming home from school this afternoon, Mason takes his usual seat in the back of the bus, beside the fire extinguisher. For a long time, he holds his head against the trembling window, eyes closed, trying to remove his memories. When he opens his eyes, he sees a small house, set back from the road, with a porch surrounded by bright beds of viburnum and phlox. A boy is walking up the steps onto the porch. He pauses at the top to strip a bunch of petals from a branch, then lets them go and watches as the wind distributes them in a roving pattern across the yard. There is a long moment during which the petals scatter, twirling.

He's kneeling on the back seat with his face pressed against the glass, which starts to rattle as the bus shifts into gear. A wind is blowing in the valley, billowing the white lace curtains in the windows of the little house and flipping all the green leaves in the trees so that they catch the sun.

The driver says, "Sit down."

The little house grows smaller until it dissolves into a row of similar homes stretching down into the valley. Now, the bus begins to climb the first hill, and the whole scene disappears behind a screen of oak and poplar.

"Sit down!"

Mason scrambles off his seat and starts to stagger drunkenly up towards the front. He has a feeling in his chest like long tongues licking at his swollen heart.

"I have to go back. I forgot something."

"I can't turn. They won't let me take you back."

The bus jerks to the left—its front wheel drops into a pothole that is deep and hardened at the edges—and its quaking frame throws Mason down onto the nearest bench.

He knows that he's close to home because the bus is moving uphill, not fast but steadfastly, keeping pace with his rising anxiety.

Sitting up, he sees the old familiar rock. It looks much different to him now; its edges dulled, graffiti faded in the rain. He knows that there has been a change in him, and now he feels that this change must have also happened to the mountain. He imagines that the air is thicker. The pattern of the bus's rattle over every stone and pothole rings untrue.

He leaves the bus reluctantly, fighting hard against the urge to turn and run back down the drive. He senses more than sees his father waiting for him, sitting on an upturned bucket just outside the kennel door, his fingers tangled in his stiffened hair, his open shirt blown out around him in the breeze.

The bus gears grind, and Mason hears it start to roll back down the hill, away from him, back down into the valley, empty and closed.

"Mason."

Spoon doesn't yell. He speaks firmly. Suddenly, the air is still, carrying his voice like a ripple. With an arm around his stomach and his head already low, Mason goes to meet his father. He counts ninety steps between the driveway and the kennel, each one soft and soundless. Spoon lifts his head, and Mason sees his eyes are filled with blood; his face is pale as vinegar.

He says, "You tried to starve my dogs."

Mason slips his backpack off his shoulders and lets it drop onto the ground. He keeps his mind filled with the image of the boy, the falling flowers, and a kind, imaginary hand that beckons to him from the little house's open window. Just this single sight has made everything different, though he doesn't know if he has changed or if it is the world that has changed around him. Staring down into the packed dirt at his father's feet, where he can see the scalloped edges of a buried shell jut from the clay, he finds the courage to say, "They ignored me..."

Spoon's thick leather boots twist inward in frustration.

"It's up to you to make damn sure that never happens."

Mason has an answer. He can feel it blowing up like a balloon inside his chest. But it doesn't explode. It only expands and grows heavier until he cannot speak at all. Spoon stands up and opens the kennel door, and Mason steps through into the wet smell of leaves and concrete, the warm humidity of twenty breathing bodies.

Now, at least, he has his answer. It is not the world that has changed.

CHAPTER 9

VALLEY

From his bed beside the bookcase, Sonny watches Trevor work. He's constructing a new model rocket using pinewood and a length of PVC he found beside the creek. He sands the nose cone, stopping every now and then to hold it out so that the dog can check his work.

Hem has shown him how to change the pressure bandages and how to crush the pills in peanut butter so the dog will take them. He lets Trevor do the nursing so that he has time to think about Kate. She left long before the sun came up and long before Hem woke from an exhausted sleep to find her gone. She left a scrap of paper by the stove, upon which nothing had been written.

"You chased her away," Lorraine says. She's wearing one of Kate's old sweaters, gray and formless. Her hair is still slicked back and glossy from the shower.

Hem is at the sink, preparing tea. Lately, it's all he ever seems to do. He mumbles, "She was going anyway."

Lorraine says, "You don't know that."

But the truth is that he does. If he stares long enough into his cup of tea, concentrating on the twisting leaves, or out the kitchen window at the place where all the pine trunks merge into a single block of green, he finds that he can lose himself inside his daughter's mind. She *is* in love; it doesn't matter to her whether she's in love with a man named Connor Biel or only with his truck, which idles just a few yards down the road, its engine laughing in the predawn dark, its tires disappearing into the mist. She loves the thump her bag makes in the truck's bed and the sound of muted country radio as she climbs up into the cab. When Connor asks if she is sure, she nods and spends the next few minutes staring through the foggy windshield, thinking of her father back at home, awakening, tired and confused, and slowly sipping his tea.

The kettle whistles, and Lorraine shoves him aside and takes it from the stove.

"I'm tired of you drifting off like that."

"I never yelled at her. I never told her what to do. I never made her go."

"I know."

She goes into the living room, where Trevor holds his rocket out before him on a string. Its metal fins are much too heavy. They have pulled the rocket's center of gravity almost into its tail.

"Cardboard?" Lorraine suggests.

"It isn't strong enough."

"Well, if you wait until your birthday, maybe we can get you one from the store."

The rocket slips its noose and clatters to the floor. Trevor looks at Hem, who is bringing in a bowl of water for the dog.

"That's not the point," Hem says. "He wants to make it himself."

Lorraine closes her eyes and pulls Kate's sweatshirt tight around her. "Well, it might be safer."

"But no fun."

Lorraine glares at the vacant space between them. "Why don't you sleep on it?"

Trevor moves the string back towards the rocket's tail and lets its nose cone dip and spin. Sonny tenses up and follows its uncertain path intently.

Later, in the silent kitchen, they avoid each other. Outside, the cicadas start their rhythmic hum. By this sound, Hem knows summer has truly arrived, with all its heat and all its insects, and especially its long, uneasy nights, throughout which they will both lie naked on their bed, their windows open to the breeze, keeping carefully apart from one another as they sleep.

In spring, a time when the unmentionable smell of drying mud out in the yard is mixed with that of budding dogwood trees to form a squalid blend that infiltrates their home, and from which there is no escape, Lorraine lies awake in bed, watching out the open window for the lights of passing planes. She likes to see the small ones from the strip in Mania blink by, their lights a finger's width above the trees, as though they might at any moment dive, touch down, and carry her away. But she's more attracted to the larger lights she finds up higher, in the stars, which are attached to planes from Providence and other cities she has never seen. Across the yard, she sees the line of trees that mark the forest's edge. This line is black and frightening. She doesn't know the way to master any of the things that she imagines lurking within it. So she lifts her eyes and concentrates her gaze upon a bright red light blinking lazily between two stars. It isn't difficult for her to place herself inside the cabin of this plane, where all the passengers are eating dinner off of plastic trays and keeping watch over the land below.

Then, from the plane, she hears the hiss, which sends her back into her body, back into her head, where she can watch the white trail rising from the darkness beyond the trees. It is immediately apparent. The rocket's destination is inevitable. She tries hard to look away but finds that she is locked in this perspective. As the plane explodes, the feeling she has is a foreign one. Still, she thinks it's most akin to cowardice. Her impulse to retreat is so strong that it wakes her in a panic.

It's hot tonight, and Hem has opened the window. She can smell the remnants of the mud and dogwood wafting through the screen. On most nights, Hem is the first to fall asleep despite his endless cups of tea. Tonight is an exception. She can feel his fingers twitching underneath the blankets like a mouse. She cocks one leg and kicks him with her heel.

The bed creaks softly in response. Hem sighs, a ghostly sound in all this darkness, then says, "Is there any way you can forgive me?"

She tries briefly to remember what he is apologizing for, but finds her mind is still fixed on the rocket, on its hiss, its long blue tail.

"Of course. I'm just a little worried."

Hem stops moving. She can feel his body stiffen. "Wait," he says, "About which one?"

She tugs the blanket close around her. She's thinking of the mud and of her daughter, Kate, who will be married soon.

She says, "Hem, only you would have to ask."

CHAPTER 10

MARCH

March has found a cup of cold, stale coffee on the stove. He drinks it down in gulps, then leans under the tap to cool his swollen eyelids. Last night's bottle stands upright in the sink, empty, a crooked nail stuck hastily through its cap.

He takes the coffee with him to the back porch. It is early afternoon, and the sun shines brightly in an empty sky. As he stumbles forward, something grabs his toe and pitches him against the railing. This manages to jerk him mostly awake. When he turns around, he sees a ragged line of driven nails running up the center of the porch steps to the door. Some of them are driven flush, but the majority rise dangerously high above the boards. All of them are red and dirty, flecked with rust.

His coffee spilled; he lets the cup fall in the weeds and sits down on the steps, stretching out his legs and back. He remembers parts of his walk back from Spoon's place yesterday, and he remembers stopping at the old nail factory his father used to own long ago, before the miners drove him out.

He remembers wading through the weeds that hide its black foundation, picking through them, and filling up his pockets with nails. Clouds were gathering on the horizon, which had made him think of rain and start to worry, once again, about the house. His father built it himself and cared for it like a living thing, painting and shingling, clipping and mowing until it seemed a breathing consciousness, content to sit on its small rise and watch dispassionately over all the land below.

But that was long before the river started its annual rise. This year, March was meant to line the cellar and drag the heavy diesel pump down from its blocks. Ever since Cathleen died, he has let the house go. He's scared of what will happen if he lets the water rise until it reaches the wood. A week ago, when the river started rising, he moved his store of whiskey to the cellar to remind himself to check for seepage. Last night, this was his undoing. He doesn't remember driving the nails into the porch or why he meant to do it. He has only a dark image of the hammer hurtling from his hand, arcing through the rain and disappearing in the tall grass. He supposes he had meant to fix things.

Now, he tells himself that he should go down to the cellar to make sure he did not make things worse. Leaning down to throw open the large steel doors, he feels a sudden pang in his lower back and has to squat to wait for it to subside. The wet earth quickly soaks through the knees of his jeans. As his forehead breaks out in a cold sweat, he begins to think that maybe he can make it back to bed, and maybe he can stay there for a while, maybe days, until he feels better. But what pride he has left won't let him follow this thought far. It brings him to his feet again and sends him grasping at the doors until they open, and, with careful steps, March descends into the cellar.

The wooden steps are dry, which is a good sign. He goes over to the shelf of whiskey bottles, takes one, and tears off the wrapper with his teeth. He's happy when the first sip slips down without incident. Lately, he has had some trouble swallowing, as though there is a clog in his chest. At times, he has to stamp his feet and shake his body like a sieve. His head is loose and foggy. His chest is tight, as though someone has circled it with heavy rope. He thinks instead of how far he has fallen.

Once, when he was younger, he had something of the confidence that comes with privilege. He supposes he still has it now, despite his father selling off the factory and all the subsequent years spent in poverty. He supposes that, like a taste for childhood foods, it's not something one ever loses, never mind what comes after. He remembers when the house was clean, bright, and solid as a ship. His father kept a flower garden, where they would eat ham and chicken salad sandwiches on summer afternoons. When he was younger, March determined he would bring the family back to riches, but in time, he let this dream die alongside all the rest. He will settle for keeping the house afloat.

The big pump sits in a dark corner of the cellar, sulking in its long disuse. To get to it, he must traverse a shallow puddle forming in the middle of the floor. He looks down at his boots, which are calfskin, faded to the color of sand. They were a present from Cathleen, but he tells himself that he has worn them for so long they no longer remind him of her. He splashes through the puddle and stands staring warily at the pump. He has not yet burned the wool from his mind, and though he thinks hard, he can't remember how to start it. He bends down and searches out a bunch of wires leading from the crank start to the engine. They feel loose, and so he rips them out and flings them in the puddle behind him. The whiskey has begun its work, and suddenly, the world seems more real. He can hear the birds singing outside, the rush of wind in the tall grass, and the gurgle of the river's steady stream.

He knows he has let the house go. He decides that if the water comes, he will pack his bags and let the river have it.

CHAPTER 11

PLAYGROUND

At recess, he immediately looks for Trevor.

Even with the cup of coffee he snuck from his mother's nightstand, it's impossible to hide the fact that he's exhausted.

Trevor says, "Your dad made you sleep in the kennel again?"

"I told you I like it."

"Yeah. You hate dogs."

"I don't mind. It's quiet."

Trevor looks away towards a group of other children playing tag. It is a clear day, and their snaps and sneakers shine.

"I'm almost done with the rocket," Trevor says.

"Yeah?"

Mason is happy with the change of subject.

"It looks good but doesn't balance right just yet."

"Which end?"

"The back's too heavy."

"So make a bigger nose."

Trevor shakes his head.

"No, it has to be a certain shape, so it just has to get heavier."

Mason squats and starts playing with a stick.

"I don't know. Put some buckshot in it."

"What?"

Trevor jerks his head around, and Mason looks up, confused.

"Buckshot," he says again.

Trevor squints. "Where am I gonna get buckshot?"

"Your dad doesn't have some?"

Trevor looks away. "I don't know."

On the other side of the playground is a wooden ship sunk neatly in a sea of shredded rubber. Children run around it, lapping up against its hull.

"Shit," says Mason. And immediately wishes that he'd kept his mouth shut. But it's too late. Trevor has already seen it.

"It's Lily!" he says.

Mason stands up, searching his mind hurriedly for a way out.

"Listen," Trevor leans in close. His stare makes Mason think of how his father looks at dogs, as though deciding what to ask of them. And he thinks that his own reaction must be how the dogs feel, frightened that the question will be one they cannot understand.

"You said you'd talk to her. You can't go back, now."

Mason shrinks a little as Trevor latches a hand around his elbow and begins to push him on his way. "How hard is it to ask a question? Just do it already."

The girls have begun to show their interest in the boys' conversation.

"Say you like her dress," Trevor says. Her dress is pale and yellow, the color of a flycatcher's breast. "Go on, the bus is coming soon."

Mason starts to walk, his anxious mind seeming to wander before him. Lily watches him approach and, when he's only ten or twenty steps away, says something to her friend, who nods and runs off towards another group.

Her eyes are blue-green, almost brown. For a moment, Mason stands by silently, hoping she will be the first to speak. Two boys run by, pelting one another with handfuls of gravel. She turns aside to watch, and Mason studies the transparent hairs that line her cheek, the dry skin on her lips, and the calm way her lashes press together when she blinks.

When she turns back to him, she has one eyebrow raised.

He says, "I like your dress."

She's quiet, staring off at something over his shoulder. Then she says, "I like you, too."

There is a smear of graphite dust along her nose. Mason reaches out and rubs this smudge away because it's at least something he knows that people do. It is strange to touch a person other than his parents. He feels a thrill that he cannot explain. Her head tilts at his touch, and her eyes go wide and dumb.

He says, "I love you," and feels guilty, both because he sees Trevor's jaw drop, as though what he said is somehow both surprising and wrong, and because Lily lifts her chin and stares at him. He can tell she thinks he has done something selfish, and he can't ever take it back.

It is a fact that all enduring loves eventually are adulterated. They are like a perfect view, a virgin landscape that completes the addled mind's unfinished sentences and makes it whole again. But over time, the weather changes, and its once-sure meaning grows more meaningless until the lover starts to wonder if the image they first saw was ever there at all. It is impossible to predict when this inevitable process will conclude: when love will no longer be love, but instead become aggravating distance, indifference, or hate. The changes may be sudden and destructive, or they may come creeping insidiously from the shadows. The first will almost always lead to ruin, but the second, just as often, will progress, and then retreat, and won't complete its course in one way or the other until both the land and its inhabitants are dead.

Hem thinks time is like a river. Though it always flows from source to outlet, it has no course he considers natural. It expands in rainy seasons and in all wet weather; it retreats whenever it's starved of itself. It's often held up by a logjam or an eddy, often turned aside and tossed back, run to ground, or swallowed up or siphoned off to serve another purpose than its own. The only certain thing is that it will eventually spill into the sea.

He stops to watch his son and Sonny cross the creek together. Trevor stretches carefully from stone to stone while Sonny splashes back and forth, snapping at the droplets flying from his feet.

Despite some early showers, the day has turned out sunny and exceptionally warm. Hem walks above his son and Sonny on a narrow plank bridge. He's thinking suddenly, against his standard judgment, that, at times, things work out for the best.

He thinks it's good that this dog, which two weeks ago was lying in the corner of his living room half-bled and shadow-eyed, is now high-tailing up the creek bank, stopping on the ridge to see if they are following. He must acknowledge that if the dog had not appeared as it did—if he had seen it in a local shelter, or if it had been admitted to his previous practice in Providence—he might have chosen to euthanize it rather than subject it to the necessary, painful treatments.

Hem reaches down a hand to help his son scale up the muddy bank. Upon the ridge, the dog whines once and disappears. This is the loudest sound that Hem has heard him make since he and Kate carried him from the barn.

"I don't see Sonny," Trevor says. He slips and slides in rubber boots at least one size too big.

"He's gone over the hill." Hem helps his son onto the bridge, and they continue up the path together, their fingers swaying and touching one another now and then.

"He's a good dog," Trevor says.

"They're all good."

"Not the ones you killed."

Hem stops.

If he were honest, he would say that this was different—that he didn't save the dog because he thought it was in the dog's best interest, or the family's, or his own—if he were honest, he would say he saved it simply because, at that moment, there was only one.

Instead, he reaches out instinctively towards his son, who flinches.

Hem steps back. "Why are you acting like I'll hit you?"

Trevor trudges on, and for a while, both are silent.

Hem says, "We've talked about this. Animals can't be bad. Only people."

He can see his son's thoughts moving and is proud of how he thinks. It doesn't matter that he never seems to come to fast conclusions. Hem knows these will come in time.

They cross the ridge into a wash of sunlight. On the far side, Hem can see George Eubanks' farm, covering the valley like a model. It is all green grass and tiny buildings, each one built with a clear and simple purpose. This is what Hem thinks he wanted—a life that is inevitably true and honest, where the natural world is a thing to fear and to revere—where all the stakes are set and do not ever move.

He bows his head and thinks that he had better try to change the subject.

"You still haven't said what you want for your birthday."

"Is Kate coming?"

Though the party is still months away, Trevor's thoughts have long been taken up with planning. He's already invited all his school friends, a few of Kate's, and two middle-school girls who work at the pharmacy in Cavalcade. Hem hopes enough of them will come to save his son from disappointment.

Kate called late last night. Because Hem couldn't think of anything to say, he waited until she began to stammer and then handed off the phone to Lorraine. Later, on the verge of troubled sleep, he stared out of his bedroom window at the ridgeline, thinking how much different distance is in life compared to dreams.

"I don't think so," he says. "No. Not anymore."

Scanning carefully, Hem finds the dog crouched at the tree line, its attention focused on the Eubanks' cows.

"There he is. Let's go."

As soon as they start down the ridge together, Sonny breaks his cover. When it's apparent that the cows do not see him or do not care, he slows and starts to slink around them in a ragged circle.

Hem leads Trevor out across the field, along a path that runs beside a drainage ditch filled with runoff from the mine. Its orange color makes Hem feel, just for a moment, as if he's living on another planet.

Sonny and a Guernsey cow are staring at each other in the middle of the field.

"Call him," says Hem, and Trevor does. His voice is shrill but gains authority from being an anomaly in a broad field of silence. Sonny pauses for a moment, staring down the cow, then turns and starts back towards them. He's running all out, and Hem feels a kind of comfort at the sight of all that wild muscle and the locomotive huff between caged teeth.

The dog runs straight at them until he's halfway across the field, then plants his feet and cuts off to the right, in the direction of the Eubanks' house. George's daughter, Mica, has just stepped out on the patio. She holds a cardboard box in one hand and a pair of heavy garden shears in the other. When she bends to say hello to Sonny, he ignores her and goes straight for the box.

"Must have something good in there," Hem says as they enter the yard.

"Just tomatoes."

She wears beige canvas trousers and a faded men's shirt. She keeps her eyes on Sonny, who is sitting down now, panting hard.

"I'm sorry," Hem says, "We haven't had the time to train him."

"That's all right."

Mica is Kate's age, and Hem has never noticed until now how similar youth makes them. Despite the many differences between their personalities, there is no way to ignore the same uncertain flicker in their eyes and the same wary arrangement of their neck, shoulders, and hips.

"We found him," Hem says. "He's still thin. He'd eat anything about now."

"Not tomatoes," Mica says.

"Try him."

She takes a tomato from the box and holds it up so Hem can see.

"Maybe smaller," he says.

She laughs and kneels down with the box. Her hair falls down around her face. Sonny takes the tomato from her hand and eats it.

Trevor says, "We came to see the bull."

Mica looks up at him, smiling. "Eustace?"

Trevor nods.

"He's in the barn." She glances at Hem. "But I think my dad's inside. I'll send him over when I find him."

George keeps Eustace in a shed beside the house, separate from the long, steel-sided barn in which he keeps his cows. The shed is painted fire-engine red with white trim, colors George says make the bull feel most at home.

Trevor runs ahead with Sonny, leaving Hem to stroll along alone, imagining the scene when Mica finds her father, maybe in the milk barn, mixing feed or helping clean the hoses. George will be a little tipsy but not worse for wear. He will ignite the chaff between his palms into a sudden golden blaze and swagger confidently over to the shed, where Hem and Eustace wait. He will be thinking quietly of simple things—the early summer heat, the foreign car he saw in town, some local gossip he has heard—all things that he will want to talk about before he ever gets to cattle, and all long before he ever comes around to what is wrong with his prize bull.

For now, the shed is silent. Hay spills from a small loft overhead, and various tools hang neatly on the yellow walls, interspersed with oil paintings of the bull's forebears. They are identical, apart from the occasional brown forelock or black nose. Eustace stands at rest inside his pen, apparently uninterested in his own distinguished ancestry.

"Come here," Hem says to Trevor. They stand silently, attentive, watching the big bull's chest heave.

"See the eyes? That's where you'll first see something wrong. People only look for cloudiness or cataracts, but there's more to it than that. You have to look more carefully."

"Did you see Sonny? He ran off."

Hem runs his palms over the bull's neck, then over its shoulder and down the prow of its chest.

"He'll turn up."

Trevor goes on through the shed to the other side, where the glossed doors stand open to the breeze. He sticks his head around the jamb and calls the dog. They hear the distant sound of a whine, impossible to locate. Trevor sets off after it, still calling, though he knows it won't help.

Hem continues his examination. By the time George arrives, he has already circled twice around the bull and stopped beside its head again, considering his own reflection in its murky brown eye.

George Eubanks is a big man, and his brash and crowding personality overstates his size. He holds a plate of thick ham sandwiches in one hand. From the other hangs a pair of long brown bottles.

"The doctor finally arrives! I thought you'd at least hit the gas for old Eustace."

Hem straightens up. "You didn't sound too concerned."

George laughs and sets the bottles down on the edge of the bull's pen. "Not like he hasn't been sick before. But you know how I love him." He squints a little as he lines the bottles up beside the sandwiches. "I brought beer. Forgot you had the kid with you."

"He ran off after the dog."

"You got a dog?"

Hem grimaces. "Some bastard tried to neuter him. Looks like he got sloppy with the knife or whatever it was he used."

"Terrible," says George, clicking his tongue. "Though I can't tell you my father didn't do the same to more than a few." He takes a bottle and tips it towards Hem. "Never got sloppy, though."

Hem looks away, back into the bull's heavy-lidded eyes. He says, "You only lose their trust that way."

George drinks his beer. When he finishes, he wipes his mouth and sniffs. One nostril, jutting sideways, slowly widens. "I guess maybe he got tired of feeding pups. No vets around here anyway. Not until you showed up. Then again, there are people who just don't take care of their animals."

He nods towards the bull. "Poor boy doesn't look at me the way he should. His eyes are all muddy."

Hem's bag is open on the railing of the pen, and he already has the long digital thermometer in his hand. "I think he has a fever." He hooks the wand into the display box and holds it like a radio while he probes the bull. The thermometer reads a full degree too high. "Liked to think that it was just his allergies. He always gets them this time of year. Then I let him out one morning, and he started circling. You can't move the old boy straight unless he's being led."

"That's Listeriosis."

George drinks with one hand while the other spreads out like a caul across the bull's forehead.

"We always just called it circling."

Hem digs a bottle and a syringe from his bag. Eustace stomps and snorts when he feels the prick of the needle.

"That's right, sissy," George says. "Let Hem fix you up, now."

"Once a day for a week," says Hem, handing him the bottle.

"All right." George nods seriously. "You think he'll make it?"

"You know as much about it as I do. You could have treated him yourself."

"I don't take any chances with Eustace. Let his line die out, and I'll have my father's ghost to deal with."

Eustace swings his head towards George's voice, pulling the halter taut. Hem drinks, watching dust drift through a shaft of pale light from the open door. There are no ghosts except for those we choose ourselves.

"Hey," George says, "There's that dog of yours."

Sonny comes into the shed at full speed, skidding as he

tries to change direction on the hard floor. Trevor runs in after him, laughing, all of his attention focused on determining which path the dog has taken.

"Stop!" Hem yells.

In the moment, just before the bull kicks through the slats, Hem curses his son's blind obedience. Trevor stands a moment longer as his wide eyes widen, and his wide mouth trembles and distorts into a scream. Then his body falls, despite him, like a puppet losing tension in its strings.

George throws a rope around the bull and pulls him to the front of the pen. Hem sees him staggering against the animal's weight, catching himself on the railing as he slips into the hay.

"He caught?" George shouts, and Hem doesn't reply because his brain has taken over where his mind once ruled. All he knows now is that his son is badly hurt. Trevor's calf is swelling, rising tight against his jeans.

"How bad?" George asks.

"Just get the scissors from my bag."

Hem holds his son's leg in his hands as George kneels with the bag, scrounging among the instruments and looking much too long at everything that he pulls out before he drops it back into the bag or to the side.

"Scissors!" Hem yells. George picks up his pace. He finds the scissors.

"Keep your head on," Hem says and begins to cut the jeans away from Trevor's leg. Halfway through, the scissors slip and touch the swollen skin. Trevor screams. He starts to struggle.

"Hold him," Hem says. Then, to Trevor, "Listen, let me get this done. I'll get this done, and then we'll fix the pain."

"Okay," says Trevor. He's sapped of strength and full of rage. His eyes roll wildly at George, who holds his shoulders firmly to the ground.

Hem keeps on cutting Trevor's jeans away up to the hip.

The leg has gone pale, though not quite as pale as Trevor's foot, which has been twisted up until it almost points directly at the ground. Hem touches it, and Trevor doesn't seem to notice.

"Can you feel that?"

Trevor's breath comes faster. He shakes his head no. He has bared his teeth like a dog—small ivory chips clenched so tight his breath whistles as it tries to pass them.

"Eustace didn't mean it," George says, stooped, returning Trevor's white-eyed stare with a red-rimmed one of his own. "He didn't mean it. Don't move now. You'll be all right. He was frightened, that's all."

Hem believes he feels the foot turn cold.

"Just frightened," George says, "that's all."

Hem digs in his bag, searching for a bandage suitable enough to make a splint. There is a rustle as Sonny creeps back into the barn. Lying low, he pokes his nose past George's heels and flicks his tongue at Trevor's sweaty hair.

Trevor's teeth part, and he says, "Dad, I can't feel it."

"He's so sorry," George says. "Aren't you? See, he's sick with it."

Hem starts to wrap the leg as tightly as he can. He starts up at the thigh and works his way down towards the break. "George," he says, "Can you call us an ambulance?"

There is a wretched look in all the eyes of men who no longer believe in justice. George's face folds inward at the eyes and mouth as though he is attempting to collapse it, as though he intends to use his outward flesh to fill some void within.

"George!" Hem says.

"Hospitals?" says George, and shakes his head. "It's just a little break. It's too far. Too expensive."

"Jesus, George, just call an ambulance."

"You've set how many legs? Just set this one—what do you think you need with hospitals?"

"That's different, and you know it. Trevor's not an animal."

George laughs. His face unfolds, and he acknowledges the situation with his eyes—from Trevor's sweating forehead to Hem's trembling knees.

"You want to tell me what's different?"

Trevor turns his head aside, raising puffs of hay dust with each breath. "Look," Hem says, "Just go in and call an ambulance. I know this may be how you do things way out here, but my son—"

"Shit, 'your son'. You think you're good enough to work on my animals but not your own son. That fucking bull is worth more than your son will ever be."

Hem shuts his eyes and breathes deeply. When he opens them, he sees Sonny looking back at him and George staring intently down at Trevor staring wide-eyed at the bull, and he's filled with the awareness of a unity of minds. He sees the dog's in Trevor, in the way he grits his teeth and waits for what will happen, and in how he strives to twist his body out of George's grasp as though, if he could manage it, he would run into the brush, to nurse his wound alone in wild growths of bramble. And he sees the bull's in George, and George's in the bull. George has spent so much time in this barn, drunk or tired out, rubbing at the bull's broad head, kissing its cold snout, his arms around its neck the way he cannot ever hold a woman's—openly and unencumbered by emotion..

The foot lies stiffly in the hay. Its skin is blue and marbled now; a corpse foot. It wouldn't be here if it were not for Hem's innovative moral compass, for the thoughts and visions that have led him and his family here, so far from their past lives in Providence. But it's here, this foot, this son. He digs into his bag and fills a clean syringe with Telazol.

George bends down to set his head against Trevor's. "You be brave," he says. "There's worse than this. You'll see."

Hem doesn't have any trouble finding a good vein. He gets the needle in and out, and in a minute, Trevor's head is rocking absently aside. A minute later, his jaw goes slack.

"All right, George, hold him."

George locks his hands on Trevor's arms and looks at Hem, who nods assent. They both rock backward on their heels, George hugging Trevor's body to him and Hem pulling on the leg, stretching it until he feels no give. Then he cries out as he rolls his shoulder and directs his son's leg back into the place he thinks is true.

The foot is now back in its proper place, and Hem can already see the flush of life returning. While he kneels there, breathing over it, George goes into his bag and finds some tape to make a splint. Hem is tired but ecstatic. He believes that there is nothing he can't do.

When the splint is done, he asks George for a ride back home. He's already thinking of the cast that he will have to make.

George frowns, stands up, and shuts his eyes tight.

Hem doesn't think he can carry Trevor back across the field alone. He knows that he should call Lorraine, but he believes that she will only make a mess of things. This is, of course, his finest moment; she will never understand.

It may be only a coincidence that Mica enters just now, having heard their screams. She pauses in the doorframe, gasps, and says, "I'll call an ambulance."

"No!" George has crossed the barn and is already back to doting on the bull. "He didn't know what he was doing. You don't have to be afraid."

"Dad!"

"That's okay," Hem says, "I set it. It's okay now. But we need a ride home."

Mica stares at George. "Alright. I'll get the truck."

George and Hem attempt to carry Trevor without jostling

his leg. This is impossible to do across the broken field, but Trevor is too drugged to protest. George says, "Sorry, Hem," again and again. He says, "He wouldn't have kicked out like that if he weren't so afraid of dying."

Mica waits for them beside the truck. She does most of the loading, climbing up into the cab and guiding Trevor over all the bench seat's lumps and tears as though she's well-used to this task.

"I'll go get the dog," she says when they are finished. "You just hold him still."

Hem nods and climbs into the passenger seat. He settles Trevor's head onto his lap and waits.

Inside the truck, it's suddenly very quiet. At first, Hem is wildly impatient, turning every second to look out the window, willing Mica to return. But this can only last so long. Every impatience has its limit. This is like a storm which, having spun itself away into oblivion, disperses all its energy into the wind.

After a while, Hem stops looking out the windows and begins to notice things. There is a spot on Trevor's forehead where his sweat has plastered two fine strands of hair in parallel, running down towards his nose. He wipes these to the side, and Trevor doesn't move. In Hem's mind, he relives, as best he can, the setting of the bone. He thinks that Trevor will be pleased when he wakes up to find out that his father is the one responsible for saving him. He thinks that everyone will have a reason to be proud of him. He believes that he has done an awful lot of saving lately.

Twenty minutes pass before Hem hears the scrape of Sonny's claws behind him on the truck bed. Mica slams the tailgate shut, then climbs into the cab and starts the engine.

"What took so long?" Hem asks.

Her eyes keep straight ahead as she backs down the drive and guides them out onto the road.

"I had to make sure Dad was all right."

By this time, the sun has dipped behind the western hill-tops. The road is stippled with a break of red and yellow beams.

"I'm sorry," Mica says, "But you should never have allowed that dog to get so close."

The trestle bridge across the creek sounds like the clattering of armor as they speed across it.

"Slow down. There's no rush, now."

"Of course there is."

"Well, your father's a drunk."

The hillsides are all ragged, black, and tan. Hem knows that George has found his bottle and will take it with him to the barn, where he can be alone with Eustace. They have lots to talk about: the bull's illness, all the cows that are now scattered dumbly in the fields, the bull's sheer power and his lack of human sentiment; stupid dogs and slow kids, the whispering of rats, chipped paint, the break, what happens when one comes to life, and anything but what might happen when one leaves it. They will discuss all these things, but they'll never get around to talking about George.

"I'm sorry," Hem says.

"It's all right."

The truck sways as it slows, and they continue on in silence. There is gray mud on the windshield and on Sonny's nose, and there is gray dust suspended in the hair that fills his ears.

"Sorry," Hem says.

"It's all right."

Sonny sticks his head through the back window into the cab. His tongue unfurls like some indecipherable alien flag.

Maybe it is never possible to be entirely at peace. Perhaps this is the nature of the universe in which we live—a universe in which all things are constantly in motion: dust motes falling in the light and hay- straws twitching in the breeze, the sudden shudder of a wooden slat as Eustace kicks it in frustration, and the muffled snap as he kicks out again and catches Trevor on the shin. Nothing in existence ever truly stops. It all keeps reeling forward in a gradual decline into disorder.

CHAPTER 12

BAR

Castration was a last resort.

When Spoon picked up the dog, it seemed both calm and cowardly. It had a good build and a good coat. He imagined it would make a good stud for his little shepherd bitch. But what he saw as calm and cowardice must have been something else. Stress, perhaps, or malnutrition. Once it had a good night's sleep inside the kennel, it was in a fury to be gone. The usual barrage of threats and beatings did not work. Spoon thought that he might cut his losses and make the dog a decent feist, if nothing else.

It seemed the dog was loose and gone before Spoon heard the chain snap. It ran diagonally across the overgrown yard, trailing flecks of blood behind it. Spoon was sick to lose it in that way, leaving it both wounded and distrustful. For a few days afterward, he couldn't keep himself from seeing it in every deer, rabbit, or opossum lying stretched out on the roadside. Every morning, he would wake up with his mind still tangled from the night before, imagining the dog still lying somewhere not too far away, still dying, still too angry with him to call out for help.

It was a week before he felt he could be certain that the dog was dead and finally allowed himself to quit his grieving and forget. He did it easily once he was certain, sloughing off emotion like a snake sheds skin.

He did not believe that he would ever see the dog again. But just today, a full month later, he was passing by the Barry place, and he saw it in the pasture, trotting alongside a man he did not know.

"You knew," he says to March, who is hunched low in a sagging lawn chair. It's mid-afternoon and the sun has dulled to a pale smudge hidden behind high clouds. Flies cut through the air between them. March doesn't stand.

March lights a cigarette. "Knew what?"

"That Hem's got Sonny. That he's keeping him."

March doesn't answer right away. He inhales deeply, then exhales through his nose. "It's not like it's a secret. Whole town knows everything."

"No one told me."

March shrugs. "You've done some shitty things."

Spoon's jaw flexes. "I've done my best. Can't help how I was raised."

March wonders whether or not to say it. Spoon is unpredictable. But in the end, his urge to talk wins out.

"My grandmother used to say, 'You don't have any say in how you're raised, the same way you've got none in how you're born. It's always up to you to make yourself the man you should be."

Spoon spits. "That's nice."

"I agree with the first part. That second..."

"What about it?"

The bar backs up against a shallow ravine, where the muddy waters of the river flow past. March stares out across it, pausing, Spoon thinks, for effect.

"Everything just flows," he says. "You get caught up."

Spoon laughs. "Like puppies in the stream."

"Shut up. I'm still upset."

"You cried like a kid who lost his pocket knife."

"I was drunk."

"Yeah, you were."

He thinks about how high that river gets. Drunk or not, it wouldn't have mattered.

Spoon steps closer. "Still, that vet had no right."

"Maybe not. Maybe he just didn't want the mutt to bleed out in his barn."

He paces, kicking at a patch of crabgrass. "That's not it. He's trying to make me look

like a bastard. Like I can't care for my own stock."

March flicks ash onto the ground. "I took Lucky to him last year when she had that cough. He fixed her up all right."

Spoon lights a cigarette and blows the smoke into his empty glass. He can't seem to keep his thoughts together; he knows that it's because he hasn't had enough to drink.

"How much did it cost?" he asks.

March sighs. "You mean how much I paid?"

"He charged you something, didn't he?"

"I don't know. A couple hundred, maybe."

Spoon whirls. "You think I don't see what this is? The whole town's turning. Whispers. That cop from Mania snooping around. Now Hem gets a pat on the back for stealing a dog out of my kennel?"

March raises an eyebrow. "What's the dog matter, then? You got bigger problems."

"Exactly why it matters," Spoon snaps. "They want to drag me down, they need a hook. They see Sonny—see a hurt animal—they think they've got it."

He's pacing again. Fast now. "I can't let it stick. I've got people who owe me. I've got accounts to settle. And Hem, he's made it real easy for them. Makes himself out like some saint. He's the kind of man who'd mistake a mourning dove for a barn owl."

March eyes him. "So what are you planning?"

Spoon stops. His mouth opens, then closes. He looks down the road, empty except for dust and a parked truck with no plates. "It's about leverage. He took something of mine. So I take something of his."

"That's your big idea? An eye for a dog?"

"It's not about the dog!" Spoon bellows. Then quieter, jaw twitching: "It's about control."

March puts out the cigarette on his boot heel. "You're losing it."

Spoon straightens, lips pressed into a line. "Maybe. But I'd rather burn it all down myself than let them do it for me."

Spoon finishes his cigarette and flicks the butt into the weeds. He thinks of how the dog was following along so easily beside the other man. He wonders how he broke him. This is what concerns Spoon most because he knows that loyalty is difficult to earn and, therefore, precious. And he knows that animals will likely only give it once. The sun has warmed the pools of stagnant water in the yard, and flies are growing bolder as the wind begins to die. Spoon sneers and stands, shoving the door back with his boot.

Spoon goes behind the bar and pours a glass of gin.

"It's too hot for whiskey," he says.

March pulls up the nearest stool and sets his feet down on the rail. "Amen. I'll have the same."

"Are you sure you want more?"

"Why not?"

"I don't know. You've been a little sloppy lately."

March grins. "You mean drunk?"

"Yeah."

"Well, I thought that was the point."

Spoon clears the burn out of his throat and pours himself

another gin. He tries to see past March's eyes, which only seem to shine right back at him.

"All right," he says. "I guess you know yourself best," and he slides the glass across the bar and turns to get another for himself.

"It's been a bad year," March says.

"Yeah, I know."

Spoon finishes his drink, sniffs, and stretches out his neck and back. This is the moment of awakening, the moment when he finds that he has had enough. His muscles tighten, and his nerves begin to sing. His mind is like a trap that finally has sprung and, in its springing, caught the drifting memories of everything he meant to do today.

He says, "It's time to go."

March sits on his stool uncertainly, with one eye on the bottle and another on his dog. "Let's have another. It's a long drive back to town."

"Don't kill yourself."

He doesn't wait for March to answer. Just steps off the porch into the insect-spattered day.

CHAPTER 13

MARCH

The light in the living room comes on without his asking. He did not mean to touch the switch, but the lever of his fingers brushed it on his way to steady himself against the frame. It flickers twice, then holds. He watches the walls breathe, and believes this is proof he's alive.

Outside, the woods have gone soft. He can hear the drip from the eaves, long and inconsistent. The floor beneath his boots is spongy—warped from the steam of too many unshed storms. The couch smells like mildew and old bread. On the coffee table, his ashtray overflows. He has forgotten whether he quit smoking or only meant to.

It occurs to him that there are no pictures of Cathleen left in the house. There were only two: one above the fireplace, taken at her sister's wedding, where she wore someone else's dress and a smile that did not belong to him; the other on the kitchen wall, of the two of them at the river, where he's half-out-of-frame and she is squinting into the sun, looking for something better.

He doesn't remember taking them down. He doesn't remember most of what he's done since the week Spoon came over with that crooked grin and said he had a way out of it. March said yes because that was the kind of word his mouth could still form. "No" took more effort. "No" required teeth.

The heater kicks on with a moan, and March counts the seconds until it gives up again. Fourteen. Same as yesterday. He presses the side of his face against the cool glass of the window and closes his eyes.

He dreams—not vividly, not even fully—but shallowly, like a man keeping one eye open. In the dream, the house is filled with water. Chairs float past him. A dog swims lazily down the hallway. Someone calls his name, but it isn't Cathleen. It's the voice of a woman he never met, calling from a place he's never been.

When he opens his eyes, the room is unchanged. Still damp, still still. He sits down and peels the label from a bottle he doesn't remember finishing. His stomach makes a sound like metal settling. He tells himself he should eat. Then he tells himself he shouldn't.

A wind passes through the house that should not be possible. The windows are shut. The doors locked. It's the kind of wind that seems to come from inside the walls. He listens to it, hoping it will tell him something he hasn't already heard.

For a moment, he tries to picture the road to Providence. It's been years. He can't remember where the turns are, but he remembers the color of the signs. Green, with white letters. Comforting in their authority.

He says aloud, to no one, "Maybe I'll go next week."

Then he stands up, checks the stove for a pot he might have left burning, finds nothing, and goes to bed.

It is four-thirty.

CHAPTER 14

PLAYGROUND

Mason's first kiss happens after school, inside a tiled alcove near the teacher's lounge. This alcove began its life as a closet, which was later converted into a girls' restroom. Much later, it was forgotten and became an unused area in the winding stream of red brick and linoleum. The kiss is quick and fumbling. They are too entangled in their desires and fears. When they are finished, they hold hands, and this is better. Somewhere outside, a door opens, and the shadow of a person passes by.

Lily asks, "Does your dad really sell drugs?"

"Yes," he says.

He doesn't think this is a lie. There have been nights when he has seen his father sitting at the kitchen table smoking, drunk, surrounded by a ring of dirty, bearded men who talk in voices either hushed or crowding. He has seen these men dig up the yard beside the kennel in the rain while his father looks on, and as he counts the seconds between thunder claps and lightning flashes, he waits breathlessly to see his mother outside in her nightgown, staring out across the hills.

Lily's hand begins to sweat. She says, "You said you loved me."

He says, "Yes," because he did.

"I love you, too." Her face is even whiter in the alcove, and in the blue light, he imagines that they are together underwater.

It is a mistake to think of life as a contest of intelligence. It is a game of individual choice–there isn't any winning–people's adoration only makes it seem that way.

CHAPTER 15

GEORGE

George Eubanks sits at the table by the big east-facing window, bathrobe open, legs crossed, rocks glass sweating rings into the wood. Mica clicks away at her laptop like it might produce heat if she types fast enough. She hasn't spoken in twenty minutes.

"You know Connor's girl's knocked up again," George says, swirling his glass. "Kate something. The mouthy one. You know the one."

Mica doesn't look up. He smirks, nods to himself. "Hell, you probably went to school with her."

She adjusts the screen. Nothing else.

George takes another sip—cheap whiskey in a better glass. He's out of the good stuff, but the glass makes it tolerable. The morning light slides across the tiles like it's trying not to wake anything.

"She could've had her pick, too," he goes on. "But no, she picks Connor. And now they're playing house out on the ridge like it's not gonna fall right down around 'em. Makes you wonder what goes on in their heads."

He leans back in the chair. It creaks under him. He likes that sound. Proof the house still notices he's in it.

Mica pulls her sleeves over her hands. He notices the fray in one cuff. He doesn't comment.

"Lorraine came by last week," he says, almost to himself. "Didn't stay long. Brought cookies or a pie or whatever. Left before the second drink."

Mica closes her laptop slowly as he lifts his second glass in a half-toast.

"She's always been decent. Little nervous, maybe, but decent. Unlike half the folks around here. Bunch of snakes wearing neighborly faces."

Mica stands.

"Are you going out?" he asks. "Or just tired of this old man?"

She hesitates in the doorway. "Neither."

"Well, pick one," he says, and grins.

She leaves.

George sits back, glass held loosely in his fingers. He watches the condensation roll down and soak into the wood. Outside, the hedge looks too perfect. He makes a note to ask someone to trim it wrong on purpose.

The phone buzzes once on the counter. He doesn't move.

"Damn place is dying," he says to no one. "And everyone's pretending not to notice."

He lifts the glass again. It's half-empty now, which he finds comforting. Half-empty means there's still a little left. Still time.

He mutters, "I swear, if Mica ever learns to lie properly, she'll be dangerous."

Then he laughs—just once—and drinks the rest. He lets the glass settle on its side, watching it roll, then stop.

Medicine, of course, is both the diagnosis and the cure. It

sometimes seems like an illusion when the cure's effectiveness is obvious, and yet the reasoning behind it seems elusive—tangible, approachable, but just beyond one's grasp.

Chapter 16

Doctor

Spoon believes that doctors are no better than magicians.

The people in the towns on the peninsula did not have access to a doctor until recently when Spoon decided he couldn't afford to make his weekly trips to Providence to purchase drugs. He did not like the long trips or the hours waiting for his shipments to arrive. He did not like the inconsistencies of traffic, cops, and weather. So, instead of buying drugs, he bought a man—a doctor and aspiring psychiatrist named Cole.

When he found him, Cole was struggling. A young man from a poor family in Providence, he was too proud of his accomplishments (and too ashamed of his past) to function in the city of his birth. He had rented a small basement office near the river, which was always cold and damp. Spoon guesses that he made the best of it for a while, at least. But by the time he found him, all the services Cole provided were strictly off the books. Prescription fraud, insurance fraud, unlicensed surgery, late-term abortions—everything is done quickly and without question. He was looking hard for ways out. All he needed was a nudge.

At first, their partnership seemed just as profitable, serious, and symbiotic as Spoon had imagined it would be. Cole did what he was told. He ordered all the pills that he was asked to order. Otherwise, he stayed out of the way. But over time, Spoon came to notice things. For instance, Cole doesn't place much value on money. He often treats his patients free of charge. On more than one occasion, Spoon has given him less cash than he's owed. Cole takes the bills regardless, stuffing them inside his desk drawer with the others.

At times, Cole asks for things from Providence. Most often, books with subjects ranging from philosophy to mathematics to religion. On distinct occasions, he has asked for California poppy seeds, a thirty-pound block of clay, mercury, magnesium, and lye.

For these and other reasons, Spoon is wary when, unasked and uncommanded, Cole calls to say that he has found a pure-bred Pharaoh hound.

There have been many nights when Spoon has sat up studying the picture in his breed encyclopedia. He loves the tailored ears, the sculpted neck, and the chiseled snout. The muscles swell up inside a military coat. He has decided that there is no dog better suited to accompany the name Sullivan.

The lighting in the doctor's empty waiting room is criminally bright. Spoon squints and listens for Cole's voice above the steady humming of the air conditioner. The shades are drawn, and the front desk is covered with a plastic sheet. He starts to wonder if he was supposed to meet Cole somewhere else. As usual, the doctor did not say much when he called. He seemed preoccupied, as though the phone call was an accident. As though the dog had come to him by accident. As though he stumbled on it, lying in a gutter near the street.

Spoon wipes his forehead, then continues through the

waiting room and down a long hall. He moves quickly past six doors, three on either side and still cannot sense any sign of life. Annoyed, he turns around and heads back down the hallway, kicking open each door as he goes.

He hopes to find Cole. Instead, behind door three, he finds the hound.

The room is small and bare except for wire racks along the walls that hold neat rows of chemicals and medicines. Spoon's arrival scares the dog up from its makeshift bed of plastic and torn paper. It retreats into a corner, where it stands with its head slung low, watching him suspiciously.

Spoon shuts the door. He doesn't want it to escape.

He has a strange sensation as he takes the photo from his pocket. For a moment, it seems as though he doesn't know if it will be there.

When his fingers close upon it, it's like someone has given him a drink.

The photograph is badly creased, but Spoon has looked at it so many times that his mind can fill in the blanks. Upon careful comparison, he's dismayed to find several disturbing differences. This dog's coat appears slightly longer, and its neck is noticeably shorter. These could be accepted variations of the breed, but Spoon can't know. His encyclopedia does not say.

"Sit," he says.

The dog sits, though slowly and uncertainly. Now Spoon can see her belly is distended. He understands the raw, expectant smell that has been wafting through the room since his arrival. The dog is pregnant.

"Shit," he says. "I hope you are what you are."

He refolds the picture and returns it to his pocket. For a long time, he is still, just crouched down, staring at his hand splayed out upon the concrete floor. He watches as the blue veins in his hands begin to bulge, as though announcing their desire to escape, and feels the tiredness that comes from sobering.

When he looks up, the dog is watching him with curiosity.

"Come here," he says.

She stands and comes towards him, skirting, following the wall. She lets him hold his knuckles out for her to smell.

"All right. That's it."

He has begun to feel a little dizzy and a little weak. He doesn't want to let Cole see him in this state.

"Wait." He stands and searches down the shelves until he finds a bottle of Desoxyn. There are only three pills left inside. He takes them, swallowing against their dryness, wishing he had something wet to wash them down.

And then there is the sorrow of desire thwarted. Everything that seems important at the moment is lost, and with it, in the void it has created, everything that ever was important or that ever will appear to be.

When Cole arrives, he finds Spoon fast asleep. One hand is resting on the dog's head, and the other is in his pocket. He's in the middle of a restless dream about the men from the church, who pop from every shadow, plucking their incessant songs about death.

Cole notices the empty bottle jutting out of place and nudges it back into line.

"I thought you'd be a little more excited."

Spoon begins to mumble something unintelligible. He shakes his head and kicks the dog away from him.

"Be careful," Cole says. "She's pregnant."

"Don't you think I fucking know that?"

"You were kicking her, so I assumed you didn't."

Spoon leans back and stretches. He's feeling better now. Revived. He clears his throat and spits at Cole's immaculately polished shoes.

"You'll have a litter of them soon," Cole says.

"Is this it? Her? The Pharaoh?"

"She's the only one around."

The dog is standing anxiously beside the door, her tail between her legs.

"You get her from a breeder?"

Cole nods. "Had her shipped. She came with papers. Let me see." He searches in the pocket of his coat until he finds a folded envelope. "I didn't verify them, but I'll do it if you like."

Spoon shakes his head. The papers are an indistinguishable mess of signs and symbols—DNA codes, lineage charts, and lengthy paragraphs in Latin. He considers them in silence, which is lent a certain urgency of purpose by the dog's incessant panting. Finally, he sighs, refolds the papers carefully, and puts them in his pocket.

"How much did she cost?"

"Not much. It doesn't matter."

Spoon stands and flexes, feeling the rush of serotonin as the drugs begin to take effect.

"Just take it out of next month's cut," he says.

Cole waves this off as though he has no plans to take what he is owed, and Spoon knows that he really doesn't care. He really won't take the money. Spoon's thoughts, usually ordered and exact, are jumbled up with one another, crossing and colliding with each other like trains in a depot full of broken switches. He believes he needs to leave. He needs to be alone. He needs a drink.

"She doesn't look so good," he says. "Looks like she might be sick."

Cole shrugs. "I'm not a vet. But you could take her to Providence."

Spoon stares at Cole and clenches his teeth. He takes a couple bottles of Desoxyn from the shelf and scoops the dog into his arms. As he walks down the hallway, through the waiting room, and back across the lot to where his truck is parked, he wonders if he should allow the dog to give birth, knowing that the puppies might come out more mixed than she is, or if he should simply end the whole thing now, while it's all still wrapped up in one manageable package.

In the end, it is his confidence that saves him. He'd like to think that he has not been duped, so he shuts his eyes, breathes deeply, and thinks about it.

In his pocket is the tattered picture of the Pharaoh hound. He tears it up and stuffs the pieces in the tailpipe of his truck.

Chapter 17

Trevor

It has only been one day since the bull, and Trevor has spent so much time in pain that he no longer takes it seriously. He can feel it, but because it is invisible, he has begun to doubt that it is real. If he lies still enough, if he imagines hard enough, he thinks he can forget. He thinks he can believe that he has never been hurt at all.

His mother sits beside him, as she will continue to do late into the night, long after she believes he is asleep. His father comes in often to twist the cast from left to right and asks if it still hurts. This is already something Trevor dreads because it does hurt, terribly and deeply, but he can't bring himself to say so.

Earlier, he heard the sounds of angry voices coming from his parents' room. They spoke in whispers, so he couldn't understand the words, but he could sense his own name now and then and knew that they were talking about him. He was upset and did not want to make them angrier, and so he lay as still as possible. He counted the mosquitoes as they slapped against the screen. It was a long time—twenty-five or thirty slaps—before the voices trailed away and died.

So Trevor shuts his eyes and drifts. He thinks about a game that he and Kate once played. She called it "Secrets." She'd hold his head between her sweaty hands, stare deep into his eyes, and say things like, "You climbed into the barn loft even though Dad told you not to." "You stole matches, and you used them to burn ants." "You have a picture of a girl from your school all folded up inside your bedpost." "Sometimes you don't think you'll ever have a friend." "Sometimes you think everybody hates you."

He doesn't know how she knew these things, but he prefers to think they shared a special bond, a kind unique to siblings. Though he was embarrassed, he would always let her start the game again. He thought it was the only way she had of understanding him.

Kate's face was always very grave. She took the game more seriously than she had to. There was only one time he remembered when her stern expression softened, falling suddenly from concentration to surprise.

"You little prick," she said. "You don't even have to worry, do you?"

This is the kind of thing he knows that he will inexplicably remember for the rest of his adult life.

CHAPTER 18

LORRAINE

Lorraine is sure something is wrong with Trevor. When Hem brought him home, she saw a bright sheen in his eyes, which she interpreted as fear that he wouldn't receive proper care. She took one look at his swollen leg, purpled down below and pale above the break, and told Hem they should go straight into town to see the doctor. But Trevor kept on saying he was all right, even though his voice was hardly strong enough to hear, and Hem seemed set on seeing what he did as an accomplishment instead of a fault. Even now, they both keep telling her that it has only been a day, that broken legs are bound to hurt, and that it will heal all right with just a little more rest. She doesn't argue with them much because she knows that they are worried, too. Privately, she prays for some sure sign that Hem has done a bad job: nerve pain, infection, or thrombosis, anything to force him to admit that he was wrong and get the leg set right. She's tired of the way they all keep hidden from each other, nursing their false hopes pathetically, like drunks with their bottles.

Trevor sleeps lightly and turns his head away whenever she attempts to touch his brow. It's a hot day, and the room is very bright, filled with the erratic sounds of insects. Small brown beetles are crawling on the screen, and spider bites are visible on Trevor's arms and neck. Beneath the sheet, his body seems unusually delicate compared to the hard bulge of his cast.

Lorraine left Kate a message telling her about Trevor's accident. She's with Connor now, which means she probably won't hear it before morning. She hopes they are happy. After she and Hem were married, they spent two weeks in a beach-side hotel built above a boardwalk full of ice cream stands and carnival attractions. All night long, the Ferris wheel turned methodically outside their window, a carousel of couples on display.

Hem was different back then, in his final year of veterinary school, and looking forward to his own clinic. He was fasci-nated by the animals he worked with and would say cryptic, sometimes unsettling things about them. That he could see the world in their eyes, that they kept him from becoming sentimental, and that they reminded him of his responsibilities as a human being. Though he never spoke of it, she knew that he expected to do great things. He was skilled at making plans, just vague enough that he would never have to measure his own progress.

Trevor shivers and sighs. She thinks of waking him to ask him how he feels. But she has done enough of that lately, and anyway, she has discovered that she likes him this way. He's perfect when he's asleep, reproduced in life exactly as he is in her own mind—kind, obliging, sweet as cream.

This past week, she has had the rocket dream almost nightly. She always wakes from it into a guilty fright, her nightgown half-translucent with sweat, and goes on tip-toe down the hall to Trevor's room. Despite the pain that warps his face, she always finds him deep in sleep. She takes a moment to observe the rhythm of his breath, watching closely for irregularities. When she's satisfied he has not finally slipped off for good, she kneels beside his bed and holds his fingertips in hers.

She thinks about her family, and most often, she concludes that she has not been a good mother. Caught up in her own cares, she has let her children grow in any way they choose, as though they are wild things that can get by on instinct alone. In the daytime, it's easy to blame everything on circumstance. She's happy when she can convince herself that she has no control and that she has always been a victim of circumstances. But in the dark, alone, she must admit that she is free. She has always had a choice, however risky, and if she did not choose rightly at the time, she has no one but herself to blame.

These nights, she doesn't sleep, which she's thankful for because she wouldn't want her son to wake up and find her nodding next to him. The way she thinks when she is with him at these times, the awful things she dreams, she can't know what terrors might be in her eyes when she awakes.

She sits with him until the dark room starts to fill with a watery gray light until the birds begin their simple chants out on the lawn, and until Trevor starts to stir as he becomes once more aware of his discomfort and pain. Then she runs, as quietly as possible, back down the hall, where she waits patiently until he calls.

CHAPTER 19

MOUNTAIN

More than almost anything, Fay hates the sound Spoon's truck makes as it pulls into the driveway. Its voice is growlingly possessive, too much like the voices that already haunt her every minute she is sober.

She runs upstairs into their room and shuts her pipe and lighter in the little rosewood box she keeps beside the bed. Then she lies down, burying her face deep in her pillow, and pretends to be asleep.

The world she inhabits now is made entirely of sound: the clean sheets whispering into her ear, the clack of Spoon's truck shutting down, the squealing of the front door, and the clopping of his boots down in the hall. She hears a skirling as something turns inside the clock beside her head. In a moment, she can feel her body lighten. In a moment, she is all unbalanced. Her feet and hips rise as her head and chest press down into the bed. She dives into it, hiding herself in it like a beetle burying itself in the sand.

And now she's asleep, and Spoon stands like a monster by the bed. His mind and eyes are blank. It could be that the pills have scrubbed him out or that the alcohol has stuffed him full.

The only thing he feels now is a fit of anger, one with neither origin nor goal. It is simple. Opportunistic. It has taken him because he left himself, and with the instincts of a parasite, it can't help but move into the space that he has left.

He takes Fay by the hips and flips her over on her back. Her eyes are shut. He shakes her, but she won't open them. When he shakes her more, she starts to babble about being stuck inside the bed.

He starts by taking off her blouse, attending to each button with tender, drunken care. Her skin is gray and slick with anxious sweat. He places one hand in the center of her chest, between her breasts, and pushes her back down into the bed, where she gives up her struggle.

Spoon folds up the blouse and stuffs it in his pocket. Now he moves on to her jeans, which he removes by small degrees, working them around her knees as carefully as if they were a part of her. As though they were no different than a squirrel's skin.

When he's done, Fay lies completely naked on the bed, apart from a thin chain she wears around her neck. He lifts her head to find the clasp, but it's tangled in her hair. He can't find the catch.

He wraps the chain around his wrist and tears it free.

Now stepping back against the wall, Spoon stares down at his wife. Her face is turned away from him. Her blackened toes point straight up at the ceiling. As he watches, she sucks in a massive breath and flips onto her side, curling her body up into a ball.

Now she is asleep. She's still, but she is breathing. Spoon tries hard to think of a single thing about her and cannot. He stands there, staring down, until he starts to feel uncertain whether either he or she exists. And now, not knowing what to do, he leaves and locks the door behind him.

CHAPTER 20

VALLEY

If Hem and Spoon were ever to meet one another on truly common ground—one of the necessarily demilitarized zones of social interaction, like a pocket in the rubble of a fallen city or the slowly filling bowels of a sinking ship—they would probably, immediately, start to talk about their families.

Spoon parks halfway up Hem's drive, engine idling rough. He lets the truck cough and clatter for a few seconds before killing it. Gravel crunches under his boots as he walks up towards the porch.

Hem opens the door just as Spoon raises his hand.

"Afternoon," Spoon says. "You got a minute?"

Hem knows just enough about Spoon Sullivan to think of him with some unease. He's heard the whispered gossip and has seen the wary glances on the street. He once passed Spoon's truck on the way to Providence, its bed filled up with plastic chemical drums. Another time, he saw it parked outside the processors' in June, with two deer in the bed and a Sheriff's deputy beside it, helping skin them out. He knows that in this place, the surname Sullivan is meant to conjure an entire history, a web of truth and hearsay that has wrapped the whole peninsula in silk. He has his mug of tea held up before him like a talisman.

"I assume this is about the dog?"

Spoon exhales through his nose. "That's right."

"He was half-dead when Trevor found him."

Spoon's slim jaw stretches back and forth. He reaches for a pack of cigarettes.

"Yeah, well, he's still mine. I've come to collect him."

They both turn, watching Sonny come around the corner of the barn. He keeps his nose down, following into the tall grass by the creek.

Spoon says, "Now I see why you all put them out. I'd swear that dog was double-jointed, the way he slipped his chain."

"You could have taken him to a professional."

Spoon laughs. It is a kind of selfless boyhood laugh. Hem can't keep himself from smiling.

"Yeah, well, at the time, I was too drunk for that."

He pulls out his wallet and begins flipping through the bills, thumbing with the special care a man takes when he knows what they are worth.

"We've had him for a while now," Hem says. "I know you want him back, but you have to understand. We're kind of attached."

Upstairs, Trevor is in bed, his leg protected only by a plaster cast. When Hem first brought him home, Lorraine insisted that they take him to the doctor. Hem insisted that a boy's leg is no different from a cow's, except that it is lighter and easier to set. He's somewhat worried that George got the best of him—playing to his sense of insecurity, his fear that he will never be quite able to protect his family on his own. But this is minor. He has almost managed to convince himself that he has done the right thing. Now, it has been almost a week, and Trevor still complains about the pain and still refuses to get out of bed and walk. All this time, it has been just the three of them, alone together, trying hard to hope.

Spoon lights another cigarette and says, "I want to say I'm sorry for your daughter. I've seen her around town with Connor."

Spoon's hand, which he draws across his mouth, is pale and clean. The smoke he exhales rides the breeze across the yard and past the creek, hanging for a moment in the wet air before disappearing in the screen of birch and pine.

"I don't know what you mean," Hem says. "My family isn't any of your business."

"I get it," he says. "You saw a dog in pain and did what needed doing. And now everyone's clapping you on the back like you're the damn hero."

"I don't know about that."

"But you know how things look. You patch up one dog, and suddenly people forget who he belonged to. Cops asking questions. Folks getting nervous. And here you are, playing the quiet savior."

"Hem steps off the porch, puts his boots in the dirt. "You think I did this to spite you? This ain't about leverage. It's about keeping something alive."

"And what do I get left with? More suspicion. More sideways looks. Like I'm the only one who ever made a mistake."

"You think this is about fairness?"

They stand in silence. The trees creak, insects hum in the background like static.

Finally, Spoon shrugs. "Keep him."

Hem nods. "I planned to."

Spoon shrugs and turns away. Halfway to the truck, he stops but doesn't turn around.

"You let me know if you get tired of him."

Hem stands watching Spoon's truck disappear behind the trees, then goes back in to find Sonny waiting for him with his head on Trevor's lap. He pours his tea into the sink, then leans against it, trying to remember how to think. He knows there is an art to it, a calm forgetting that will make a space to let it in. Opening his eyes, he sees a lump of gray inside the drain, and suddenly, the only thing that he can think of is the dead weight of a St. Bernard inside a trash bag, bumping stiffly down a flight of concrete stairs.

Lorraine says, "What did that man want?" Her lips are tight, her face drawn.

"It's not important. We can talk about it later."

"Yeah."

Trevor scratches Sonny's ear. "He didn't even ask to see him."

"Didn't need to," Hem says. "He already knows he lost."

A sharp yelp breaks the silence. Trevor jerks upright, clutching his leg.

"What is it?" Lorraine rushes over.

"It's my leg," Trevor says, his voice tight with pain. "Same place. It really hurts."

Hem kneels beside him, gently placing a hand just above the break. Trevor flinches.

"You must've twisted it," Hem mutters, though the bruising hasn't faded and the swelling looks the same as it did two weeks ago.

Lorraine folds her arms. "Or maybe it never healed right."

She waits until Hem meets her eyes.

"Hem, for God's sake. Just admit that something isn't right."

She sits against the windowsill with both arms wrapped around her. Trevor looks up from the couch, and Hem can tell that he is holding back from telling him the many things he's just told his mother.

"I don't know how many times I have to say it. Broken legs hurt."

Trevor and Lorraine both turn their faces towards the window. Hem thinks that Lorraine must hate him. He believes a day will come when she will not be able to forgive. The truth, if he were willing to admit it, is that he has never seen a broken leg that did not start to knit within a week.

"We've got to take him into town," Lorraine insists, "It isn't healing right. He needs a doctor, Hem."

Spoon is far away by now, probably halfway to Cavalcade.

"Hem," Lorraine says.

"Dad?"

"What, Trev?"

"Can we just see the doctor?"

CHAPTER 21

FAY

She wakes up naked, the sheets wound tight around one leg, the other cold against the damp edge of the mattress. Her head throbs, not sharp but low and constant, like water leaking through plaster. There is light coming through the slats. Not morning light. The hour between things.

She reaches for the edge of the bed but finds only air. There's a broken glass on the bed stand, but that doesn't bother her. What does is the absence. Of sound. Of footsteps. Of the smell of cigarettes or cheap leather. Just her breath, quick and thin, and the faint creak of the house inhaling. She doesn't remember getting into bed. Doesn't remember getting out of her clothes. Somewhere in her head, there's the rhythm of a song she knows she doesn't like, and the taste of orange juice that had been sitting out too long.

Her body feels used, but not in any way that makes her panic. In a way that makes her angry. She pulls the sheet across her chest and closes her eyes.

Her mother's house smelled like varnish and dead air. Always. Even in the summer, when Fay would prop open every window, wedge them with old paperbacks, and let the breeze run through like it was trying to escape something, too. Her mother was the kind who left meals on the stove until they went dry, who spoke in half-finished sentences and expected you to understand the rest. She'd tell Fay to wear socks, but wouldn't buy them. Would mention the dangers of men without ever warning her about one in particular. Fay remembers the night she started bleeding. Her mother handed her a book—"You'll figure it out"—and turned back to the television. Fay took the book into the bathroom and sat on the floor with her knees pulled to her chest. She didn't cry. She told herself she was learning. She told herself that silence was a kind of attention.

When Mason was born, she didn't cry then either. Not from pain and not from joy. She watched him blink up at the ceiling with that same blank stillness that her mother wore until the end. For a moment, she thought he looked just like her. For a moment, she was terrified.

But she fed him and she kept him clean. She didn't ask him questions that she wouldn't want to answer. She loved him, she thinks. Just not in the ways people expect mothers to love.

She swings her legs off the bed and stands. The air is cold on her skin. Walking to the window, she looks out at the gray light thickening over the valley. The house is still breathing. So is she. That has to be enough, at least for now.

CHAPTER 22

BAR

Spoon wants to believe that he has done a good job. He'd like to tell himself his father would have done it just the same, but he knows this isn't true. Rig would hold the vet at gunpoint, get the dog, and, when he got it, shoot it on the spot.

This is the kind of thing that Spoon would often like to do and often finds that he cannot. He tells himself what he will do a hundred times, repeating it until it seems like something that has happened rather than something that will. And yet, when the time comes to demand his action, he can't push through his fear.

Spoon thinks, perhaps, that he has lied more to himself than he has lied to others. This doesn't surprise him, nor does it disturb him. March once said that a fair amount of self-deception is essential for maintaining mental equilibrium. Spoon likes to think that this is true, but he can't convince himself that equilibrium is something he is interested in achieving.

Chapter 23

George

George Eubanks sits in the room he calls his study, though no one else does. The word is carved into a plaque above the door, hammered in sideways back when he thought that sort of thing was funny. The room smells like paper and old smoke. The windows don't open. He likes it that way.

The journal is heavy, leather-bound, thick with the weight of his thoughts. He keeps it on the top shelf behind the cookbooks no one touches anymore. Mica once asked if it was full of old recipes. He didn't correct her.

He writes slowly. His pen is fine-tipped and temperamental. He believes this gives the words more weight.

Man's natural condition is one of indulgence, he writes. All virtues are learned. Hunger, pride, pleasure—these are not sins. These are furniture.

He pauses to drink. The glass leaves a circle on the blotter. He does not blot it.

Every time someone says they're doing their best, they're lying. People only do what's easiest, or what they can't avoid.

And sometimes those things overlap, and that's what we call character.

The handwriting is erratic. He prefers it that way. He imagines scholars will one day marvel at the shifting tone; debate whether the variation was intentional.

I have never worked a day in my life, he writes, with satisfaction. *Which is not to say I haven't suffered. Comfort is no barrier to suffering. It just makes it harder to complain without sounding like an ass.*

He underlines *ass* twice.

Outside, the wind pulls at the shutters but doesn't get in. He hears it but doesn't acknowledge it. His house, like his thoughts, is well insulated.

There's a cigarette in the dish beside him. He doesn't smoke anymore, but he lights one now and then just to watch it burn. This one curls, unattended.

He writes:

If anyone is reading this, it means I'm dead, and you're either my daughter, a petty thief, or some poor bastard with too much time. In any case—hello. Hope you're comfortable. If the drink cart's still stocked, pour one for me.

He signs the bottom not with his name, but with a small, looping **G**, like a secret handshake only he understands.

The journal makes a soft thump when he closes it. He holds it in his lap for a moment, pressing the cover like it might offer warmth.

Then he stands, slow, knees complaining in their usual dialect. He returns the book to its place behind the cookbooks.

"Right where it belongs," he says aloud, and the room does not disagree.

He doesn't turn off the light when he leaves. He likes the idea of it glowing all alone in there, without him. A small, unread monument.

CHAPTER 24

DOCTOR

The antiseptic smell of Doctor Cole's examination room reminds Hem of his own examination rooms in Providence. He misses it—the sense of order it provides, compared to the smells of dander, steel, and hay. And he has forgotten how much he enjoys the way people occupy these rooms, aloof in separate corners, yet with a common interest focused on the table between them.

The x-ray shows a knot of bone, slightly off-center. Cole, a young man with a red-cheeked and grim-eyed face, says that he will have to re-break it.

"It's a pity, really. You were close. So close, in fact, I'd have to chalk it up to stress. Too bad it wasn't just a cow or pig. You obviously know your job."

Cole tries to turn the leg, and Trevor's eyes shut tight against the pain. This brings Lorraine to his side. She holds his head between her palms, massaging it the way she always does in winter when he comes in from the cold.

Hem says, "How much will it cost?"

Cole frowns. "A couple hundred, mostly for the equipment. It doesn't really matter since it has to be done. Look."

He waves Lorraine away and puts his hands on Trevor's head, where hers have been. Trevor looks up at his mother. They are emptied by fear. "There's a difference between us, animals and humans. But it's all up here. To be completely honest, I think we give up too much for this thing."

"We just want his leg fixed," says Lorraine.

Cole straightens up and looks at Hem.

Trevor asks if it will hurt.

"Just a pinch," Cole says, "and after that, not anything that you'll remember."

He turns away from them towards a cabinet of medical supplies and drugs. Hem watches as he finds a small syringe and fills it up with Ketamine.

Lorraine says, "He'll still feel..."

Hem nods. He wants Lorraine to leave. He knows what Cole will do and likes to think that she can't bear the shock of seeing. More than this, he'd like her to believe that he has earned the right to stay by virtue of the years that he has spent observing and admiring the things that other people turn away from—things that they no longer think are real.

The needle enters. Seconds later, Trevor's eyes go dull. Lorraine is up, her hands upon the door, and gently, Hem says she should go.

He reaches out to keep the door from slamming shut behind her, then helps hold the leg while Cole removes the cast. Underneath, the leg is white and green, apart from an impressive bruise around the break. To Hem, it looks like something living has attached itself. He thinks of animals with sucking tentacles, of plants with spreading crimson tendrils.

Cole says, "Hematoma." He selects a different drug and numbs the area, then starts to cut through the bruised skin.

"Hanging in?" Hem asks.

Trevor nods.

Cole drops his scalpel in the sink and opens up a drawer under the table. He lifts up a hammer and a chisel.

Hem says, "Will it hurt him?"

"Sure. But he won't know the difference."

Silently, Hem promises himself that he will watch. Because he feels his job demands it, and because he thinks that he should know what he has put his son through.

Cole slips the chisel into the incision, and Trevor screams. Hem watches, trying hard to feel the pain and growing more and more disturbed that he cannot. Just outside the door, Lorraine is squatting on the floor, her knees drawn to her chin. Her fingers are all twisted into one another, gripping hard, intent on riding it all out.

CHAPTER 25

MOUNTAIN

Now, when he returns home, it's to discover everything anew. His memories are like the memories of photographs that he has seen. They are too static, much too rigid in their form and content to be taken for reality. The house, until he enters it, stands against the sky like a stiff paper screen, hiding something shy and inaccessible. Even his own room feels like a lifeless copy of the only place where he has ever felt safe, where he has at all times felt whole. At dinner, he wants desperately to tell his parents about Lily. When he says he has a girlfriend, they both stare at each other. Even his mother, who has been only half-attentive all night.

"What's her name?" Spoon asks.

"It's Lily."

"What's her last name?"

Mason doesn't know. In the weeks that they have spent together, he has never asked.

"Got to have one," Spoon says, "Everybody does."

Mason chews as slowly as he can. Only forty paces from the door, there is the kennel, full of dogs that are now worse than simple animals that do not pay him any mind. Now they are just stand-ins, cut-outs. Now, he knows he has no chance of gaining their affection.

Mason's mother starts to nod off, and Spoon nudges her beneath the table.

"Keep your head on." Then, to Mason, "What color is her hair?"

"Brown." He says.

Spoon laughs. "That won't help."

Mason wonders if describing hair isn't supposed to be this simple. "Yellow-brown," he says, "like yours."

Spoon considers. "Fosters have a Lily, but they've all got red hair."

Mason's mother rubs her bloodshot eyes. "Everyone?"

"Hell, yes," Spoon says, "One thing breeding's taught me —there are strong genes, and there are weak ones, and red hair might be the strongest. You don't dodge red hair." He takes another bite and turns back to Mason. "They teach you this stuff?"

Mason shakes his head no. Spoon nods, swallows, and looks slyly at Mason's mother. "You have to fight anyone to get her?"

Mason automatically says yes. His father raises an eyebrow, his fork laden with green beans halfway to his mouth.

"Fighting!" says his mother.

"I had to."

"See," says Spoon, tipping his fork. "Had to." He winks and stuffs the beans into his mouth, then speaks through the smacking sound of his own chewing. "I don't see you beat up any."

He wants his father to think well of him. He has seen the world now, and he believes that a boy with a girlfriend, no matter how little he knows about her or how seldom he sees her, can't possibly be thought of as a mere boy any longer. He's something of much greater consequence. Not a man, perhaps, but still the kind of thing you do not put inside a kennel.

"It wasn't much of a fight."

"Hah!" Spoon's fork and knife drop noisily onto his plate as he gives himself up to laughter. "That's—" he chokes, pointing back and forth between himself and his son. "That's genetics. Goddamn."

CHAPTER 26

SHOKTEN

They are walking down a narrow path, flanked on one side by a line of pines and, on the other, by a low brick wall. The wall is nearly covered with Boston ivy and clematis. Two small brown birds hop along it, picking in the dirt.

Trevor hops along on crutches, holding his new cast high off the dirt. Every now and then, he glances over with concern. For the first time, Mason wonders if he knows.

Trevor says, "Are you sure this is all right?"

Mason answers, "Yes. "We'll be back before class starts. It's just a little further."

Mason notices a hissing sound coming from behind the wall. It reminds him of the sound the gas makes in his mother's oven when she forgets to light the flame. They come around a bend, and then there is the smell of burning grease and charcoal. Behind a chain-link fence, Mason sees a concrete stack. A stream of black smoke rises from it, rising up until it's cut off by unseen winds and blown back over them, across the trail and past the trees beyond.

Spinning on his crutches, Trevor pushes Mason up against the wall and whispers, "Don't let anybody see you."

Mason has one eye pressed to the wall, which, this close-up, looks like the surface of the moon. His other eye is staring at a low brick building squatting underneath the stack. There is a white van parked beside it, with its back doors open wide.

Trevor's breath is soft on Mason's neck. "I told you. This is where they burn them."

Now, a man emerges from the building and walks over to the van. He leans inside and pulls out two black bags. Struggling a little, he drags both of them behind him back into the little building underneath the stack.

"Burns who?"

"You know. The dogs."

Trevor's lips are almost pressed against his skin.

"They're in the bags."

Trevor's eyes are dancing, but Mason isn't quite sure what to say. He stares out at the two men, who are struggling to get a gurney back into the van.

"Why don't they just throw them in the woods?"

CHAPTER 27

KATE

Kate is on her way home from the discount store in Cavalcade, which she has found to be the only store on the peninsula that carries cocktail onions. She has spent all day searching for it—long enough to make her wish that Connor had not been so adamant about his birthday dinner.

In only two days, he will be twenty-one. He seems to think that this is some kind of a milestone, closer to the even quarter of the century, which he believes that he will live. A part of her would like to think he's right—that some years are more serious, more meaningful than others—but another part would like to tell him he is being dense—that passing years mean nothing, or, at least, no more than being born into the world in the first place.

It is early afternoon, and on the long road back to Cavalcade, she has yet to see another vehicle. As she curves around the next bend, she sees the Eubanks' farm and knows she's close to home. It is almost Trevor's birthday, too. She briefly thinks of asking him to share in Connor's celebration, but decides it's not a good idea. There will be a bunch of miners there, all drunk and looking for a laugh.

She's approaching the unmarked boundary between Cavalcade and Shokten. Just across the road, there is a torn place in the guardrail where she used to meet Connor, back when he had not yet asked, and she had not said yes, and they still had the force of mutual uncertainty to wire them together.

Looking out the window at this gap, her head fills with the smell of pine, the taste of soft fog rising from the asphalt. For a moment, she imagines stepping on the brake. But she recovers quickly. She has told herself that she will not be sentimental. Still, as she continues towards her new home, she's well aware of an uncomfortable attachment to her old one, which is just a quarter-mile from here, down a steep path edged with tall Virginia pines and silkgrass. She's thinking down it, following the ghostly form of her remembered self, when a doe leaps from the woods beside the road, and she collides with it, breaking both its front legs mid-shin.

Pain is not avoidable. The things that act upon us do not ask us to feel anything. If we do so, it is either because we choose to, or because we cannot help it. Either way, we are responsible for our reactions. There is no one else to blame.

CHAPTER 28

FAY

She has decided that today, she will try to remain relatively sober. She has reached a point at which no man wants her—not even Cole. Usually, she could just call Connor. He'd be over in a minute with whatever she asked. Today, his phone just rings.

She has deliberately chosen a day that should be easy for her. Spoon is spending at least another night in Providence, and she can always sit Mason in front of his books for a few hours before sending him to bed. She was worse to herself than usual last night, hoping that some comfort would carry over. When she stands up, there is no rush of pain. Her head feels light and spacious. This is good, but it is somewhat far away from what she'd hoped for.

The house is quiet, and the clock says ten. She will have to get high again before noon if she doesn't want to be stammering in bed when Mason gets home. She will have to be careful and take only what she needs to remain upright. It's a fine line between sobriety and making a fool of herself, but one she's walked before, though it has been some time.

She goes to the bathroom and showers, then puts on a clean pair of sweatpants and a shirt.

Downstairs, the silence grows louder. There are Mason's toys scattered all over the living room and a pile of Spoon's guns on the kitchen table.

She rubs her face and nearly skips the bottom step, catching herself short on the opposite wall. She's never known Spoon to keep them like that—out here on the table where everyone can see. For the most part, he has squirreled them away in secret places—atop a tall shelf, in the closet, behind his shirts—places he believed no one knew about.

The pile sits there, silently withholding any meaning.

She goes back upstairs to the cabinet beside her bed, where she keeps her drugs. She can tell immediately, by the lightness of the handle, that something is missing. When she quickly pulls the handle towards her, she finds the drawer nearly empty, apart from a few broken needles and a pack of cigarettes.

She sits down on the bed, sighs, and lights a cigarette. It is likely Spoon took it. He has done this twice before when he was running low.

She goes into her closet to a pile of old dresses in which she keeps what she thinks of as her "emergency" box. But the box is already out of place—separated, empty, and tossed into the opposite corner.

Her first thought is that this isn't like Spoon. Then it hits her—somewhere at the base of her neck, then traveling in a wave of unpleasant sensations up and over her head—the knowledge that she's dry.

This thought alone is enough to make discomfort come on fast. Her head pounds and her nose begins to run. In the past, she would have toughed it out until Spoon got home—just lying on the couch with a box of tissues. For a moment, she thinks about going back to bed, balling up and trying to ride things out. But today is different. She wants to do well. Clean the place up. Make dinner for Mason. She wipes her face, and tells herself that she will go to Cole. He'll have to help.

Outside, the sun has topped the peaks. The air is starting to heat up. A flock of starlings are chattering amongst themselves at the top of the drive. Everything seems too bright. Too loud.

She starts to walk.

CHAPTER 29

KATE

She wasn't driving very fast. Though the windshield is cracked and the hood a little crumpled, she's glad that she won't have to tell Connor that the car is wrecked.

Staring at the broken windshield, with her mind poised momentarily between its last hop and the next, she realizes something she will not remember—that the only difference between Connor and her father is that Connor has not spent enough time in close company with hardship to accept it.

Then she turns her head and sees the doe. It is struggling to squeeze its body over the guardrail with both front legs dangling against its chest, like sausages.

She fumbles at the handle, flings the door open, and steps out into the empty road. She takes a few steps towards the doe before remembering her phone, which she left lying in the cup holder. As she dials, she can hear the doe crying behind her and its front hooves scraping back and forth along the rail.

Her parents' line is busy. In a panic, she gets back inside the car and shuts the door behind her. Outside, the doe is stuck with one leg slung over the rail, its back legs trembling. It stops its crying and looks up, nose in the air, as though it has put all its suffering on hold to smell something both sweet and distant.

"Goddamn animal," she says and turns the key in the ignition. When the engine starts, she feels a heady mix of pride and shame. There is a small knife in her pocket and a set of miner's hammers in the trunk. The doe is stuck now, with the guardrail in its belly and its front hooves lying sideways in the mud.

For a long time after, she will do a good job of forgetting that she drove away. She will focus on the things that truly matter. And eventually, when she finds that she can't ignore it any longer when the memory comes back with hat in hand and begging for her interpretation, the lesson she will learn is that you can't help those who have hurt themselves by jumping in your path and that you can't waste time worrying about the future.

CHAPTER 30

MARCH

Anise Fitzpatrick is with March. They are sitting, once again, at the very end of a long, thickly varnished table at the Courthouse Buffet. They are always at the end (almost a full week running, now) because it gets them closest to the river, which is slowly soaking through the land behind the restaurant, loosening the soil, showing its advancement in the swath of yellowed grass that daily grows along its banks. It is the edge of this swath, the blurry line that separates the yellow from the green, that they have come here to watch.

Anise retired from the Courthouse three weeks ago and, since then, has been spending most of her free time at the same smudged window where she used to take her breaks. She has planned to take a long vacation with her husband, Tommy, which is really an attempt to wrap the past few years in cellophane and put them somewhere they can be forgotten.

"Think we'll still be here next week?" she asks to get March talking.

He only sighs heavily. "I really don't give a shit."

Anise stares into her coffee, which is the same cold color as the river.

"Well," she says. "I do."

She imagines that the sober March (if there ever was one) would want nothing to do with her. But she's thankful to have someone to sit with. At this point in her life, she has little patience for spending time alone.

She decides to try once more. "So what will you do if the house goes? Stay right here and wait for the insurance money, I guess."

March nods slowly.

"Tommy's sister waited over a year for hers. Can you believe that?"

"The ground was soft already," he says. "It's been that way for a while."

She can tell by the apologetic look he gives the river that he's about to bring it up again. Even though they have agreed five times, now—

"I was thinking more last night. I think they would have left us."

She shuts her eyes and breathes deeply. In the kitchen, they are starting up the grill, and the smell makes her hungry. She takes a menu from the table, even though its image is etched deeply in her mind and will remain so.

March says, "Cathleen would have left me. I'm sure of that."

"Well, then, it's a good thing time doesn't run backward."

March laughs, looking out at the river as though it has spoken.

CHAPTER 31

KATE

Kate is in her driveway, scrubbing blood and tufts of downy fur from the fender of her car. She has the car doors open and the radio playing, so she doesn't hear Fay Sullivan approaching—not until she's already close enough to touch.

Kate spins around and curses, rocking Fay back on her heels.

"I need Connor," Fay is saying, even as Kate attempts to regain her composure. She's dressed haphazardly, as though she had not expected to find herself outside.

"I need to see him before I go home."

Kate leans against the hood, hiding the bloody cloth behind her back.

"He works today," she says.

Fay looks at her dreamily. "You don't even know."

Kate stiffens. "Know what?"

"That we're the same age."

Kate is quiet, thinking, while Fay continues, muttering, "almost...almost..."

"I can have him call you," Kate says. Then, looking down at Fay's bare feet, "Do you need a ride?"

Fay stares at the car.

"That's Connor's car," she says.

Kate shakes her head. "It's mine, actually."

"He drives it."

"Yeah, he borrows it sometimes. He doesn't like taking the truck to town."

Fay nods, turning the situation over in her mind. "I just need a little," she says. "He keeps it somewhere in there."

"I don't—"

"—I just need a little," Fay says. "Spoon won't know anything."

Suddenly, Kate has the uncomfortable feeling that she knows exactly what Fay is talking about. But Fay is already moving past her, circling around towards the back of the car.

"They always keep it here."

She tries the trunk, finds it locked, and gives Kate a desperate glance.

"It's my car," Kate insists. "There's nothing in it."

Fay tries the trunk again, making the car's rear end bob lazily.

Seeing that Fay won't leave, Kate unlatches the trunk and watches her lower half as she roots around inside it. She hears the small panel over the wheel well fall away.

Fay raises her head. "You got a baggie? Or a tissue or something?"

"Listen," Kate says, "let me take you home."

"I'd just take all of it, seeing as it's mine, but I don't think Connor would be happy."

Fay laughs, then retreats suddenly from the car's interior, looking confused and frightened.

"You know not to tell Connor, right?"

After a long pause, Kate nods. She has a sickening feeling

that she only understands small parts of this life she has married into—a life, she thought once, that couldn't possibly mean anything but freedom and salvation.

Fay motions, returning to the trunk, and Kate goes to the front of the car and finds a discarded wad of cellophane. The trunk slams shut behind her.

Kate doesn't have time to remove herself from the driver's seat before Fay has slipped in beside her. She takes the cellophane and starts rummaging through her pockets.

"Are you still giving me that ride?" Fay sounds breathless.

"How far is it?" Kate asks. She stares at the dent in the hood where the deer struck.

Fay follows her gaze. "What, you never hit a deer before?"

Kate shakes her head.

"Well, that's fucking impressive," Fay says, rolling down her window to light a cigarette. "It's just through town and up the hill. You know where."

Chapter 32

Fay

Fay is feeling good—just the way she needs to. Spoon will be home soon, and Mason is probably already waiting. She knows Connor will notice what she took. She assumes the blame will fall on Kate, but that's all right. She doesn't know much, but she's smart. Fay doesn't think she will break.

"Anyway," she says out loud, "Connor's soft. He isn't like Spoon."

Surprisingly, Kate laughs. "You think he's *soft*?"

Fay reaches instinctively into her pocket, holding the twist of paper she has hidden there.

"I bet he doesn't hit you," Fay says plainly. She wishes that she hadn't started talking. She has realized, too late, that Kate isn't like other girls. She's innocent and likely to take things too seriously.

Kate tenses. "You mean Spoon...?"

"I didn't mean to say that," Fay says. "It isn't your business to know."

Kate is quiet until they are through town and have begun to climb the hill. In the meantime, Fay keeps her head down as they pass the shops and restaurants on Main Street. Her body is suddenly ablaze with emotion—the shame of riding through town with a view of this pretty girl's glove box, the fear of what will happen if Spoon comes home early, the weight of having to confess again how weak she is compared to him.

It's too much. When she gets home, she will have to heat up something for Mason's dinner. Then she'll go upstairs and try to burn these cancers out, even if it's only for a moment. The paper in her pocket buys her time—time to think, to get her head just high enough to take a look around.

As they near the top of the drive, Kate says, "I'd like to help if I can."

It's all she says. Afterwards, she falls silent.

Fay is turned towards the open door, with one foot in the gravel. In front of her, the house is backlit by the sun. She wonders what Kate would do if she asked her to keep driving —she wonders where they would go. It wouldn't matter, except that now she sees the side door open, and Mason emerges on his way to feed the dogs. He keeps his head down, focusing as though he's counting his steps.

She turns to Kate, looks her up and down, and decides that she has not had any children.

"Just don't say anything to Connor."

Kate smiles wearily and nods.

CHAPTER 33

PLAYGROUND

Mason waits for Lily in their usual spot, the tree-lined path behind the school. He's toying with a beetle at his feet when he becomes aware of rustling a few yards away. He peers carefully through the trees and catches sight of a bright white sneaker.

He should have known he'd spy. The question—Mason ducks into the bushes (he doesn't think Trevor's seen him)—is what Trevor's looking for—the thing he wants.

In front of him, a butterfly has landed on a leaf, and it is sucking dew. Of course, he knows what Trevor wants. He wants Lily. For a moment, Mason thinks that he might give her to him. For a moment, he enjoys the fact that it would be so easy. That he has this thing—this person—so indebted to him. So enthralled it's up to him to keep her or to send her on her way.

But this is interesting. Trevor's not the jealous type. Since they've been friends, he's always had the best of everything—fresh paper for his notebooks (one for every class), new pens and pencils—not to mention the rockets he's always talking about.

But now he's jealous.

Mason turns and leans against a tree, watching the end of the path where he knows Lily will eventually emerge. In his mind, it's better to have a person than nice things. A man can pay for things—that's easy—but you can't buy people. Well—he's thinking of the dogs—you can't buy loyalty. You can't buy respect.

Chapter 34

Kate

Kate drives them towards the bluff at the far edge of the valley. The road winds along the base of the hills, where the trees thin out and the sky opens above them. The air is warm but sharp. Connor leans his elbow out the passenger window, the wind fluttering the collar of his flannel shirt. He hasn't said much since they left her house.

"You okay?" she asks.

"Yeah. Just thinking."

She glances at him. "You always get quiet like this."

"You always get loud," he says, but without malice. He smiles, just a little.

She pulls into a gravel turnout near the overlook. The engine idles a moment before she kills it. They sit in the silence that follows, both watching the horizon, the last light pooling along the ridge.

"I keep wondering what it's gonna be like," she says. "When we're actually out of here."

"Better," Connor says.

"How do you know?"

He shrugs. "I don't. But it has to be."

She frowns, running her hand along the steering wheel. "You sure we aren't just dragging all the same shit with us?"

"Probably. But at least it'll be ours. Not theirs."

She bites her lip. "Sometimes I feel like we're acting like kids. Like we don't even know what we're doing."

Connor looks out at the trees. "We don't. But we know what we don't want. That's something."

"I think about Trevor sometimes. About how he looks at me now. Like I'm already gone."

"He'll understand."

"Will he?"

Connor doesn't answer right away. A long silence follows. Then, "Maybe not now. But he will."

Kate thinks.

"What if it doesn't work out?"

"You mean us?"

She nods.

He thinks a moment, then says, "Then it doesn't. But we won't be stuck here pretending it does."

She stares out at the darkening line of trees.

"Did Spoon say something to you?"

Connor shifts in his seat. "He always says something. This time it was about you."

"What did he say?"

"That you were a nice girl. And that maybe you ought to think twice."

Kate laughs, though it doesn't sound like humor. "He just wants to keep you under his thumb."

"Probably. He still thinks he can talk me into staying."

"He can't."

"No."

They sit in the quiet again, the first stars blinking into view.

"You remember when we first met?" she asks.

"At the gas station. You were buying Gatorade."

"And you said I didn't look like I was from around here."

"Because you didn't."

"Still don't."

He looks over at her. "That's why I asked you out."

She smiles.

"You're gonna marry me, Kate."

She leans her head back against the seat. "I already said yes."

"Yeah, but I want to hear it again."

She turns to face him, hair caught up in the wind through the window.

"Yes," she says.

He leans across the console, kisses her forehead. They sit there, heads bowed together, while the night grows darker around them.

After a while, he says, "You ever wonder what it would've been like if you'd stayed in Providence?"

"Sometimes," she says. "I imagine different schools, different people. Different me."

"Would that version of you still talk to me?"

"Maybe," she says. "But I doubt we ever would've met."

He shifts to face her. "I would've found you. Doesn't matter the place."

Kate laughs softly, rests her hand on his arm.

"You know," she says, "I thought I was supposed to be smarter than this."

"Than what?"

"Than falling for a guy who works at the mine, who's got a crooked uncle, who might be just as stuck as me."

"You think I'm stuck?"

"I think you're trying. And that counts for something."

He watches her carefully. "You're trying, too."

They both fall quiet again. The stars are out now, clearer

and sharper than they seem from town. A breeze rises and passes, lifting the leaves just enough to make a sound.

"We should probably go back," she says.

"Not yet."

She nods. And they stay like that, sitting in the dark, in a place that doesn't belong to anyone, where for once, they don't feel so owned by everything else.

CHAPTER 35

VALLEY

Sitting together by the creek, Kate and Lorraine remove their shoes and cool their feet in the stream, the way they always used to when Kate was small. Looking down into the water, Kate remembers almost every polished rock. She knows the loose arrangement of the tree trunks on the bank.

Her mother says, "You seem unhappy."

Kate's been waiting for a moment. She decides this might as well be it.

"I'm pregnant."

There is just a pause, a moment when the whirl of the creek goes slack.

Lorraine kicks in the water and catches Kate's toe with her own.

"Does Connor know?"

"Not yet."

"When will you tell him?"

"I don't know. Mom—"

"You don't want to have it?"

There are minnows in the shallows, nipping at her feet.

"I don't know. I don't really want to, but I can't think—I can't think of any reason not to."

Kate thinks of her father, who is no doubt inside, drinking tea and watching them, his face a phantom, hidden by the light that glances off the kitchen window. She thinks of Trevor, who is calmly planting colored pennants on the lawn, only to get angry as the wind picks up and blows them down. She wonders if these two will ever have to worry in the way she does—if they will ever find life so confusing or so hard.

Lorraine says, "I suppose I should know better. But the truth is, that's the only reason I've ever done anything."

By now, Kate is familiar with the way that Connor looks when he comes home from work. He has his first, second, and third drink, and he moves about and handles things— his silverware, his glass, the finicky antennas on the television—as though he's afraid of them, as though he doesn't really know what they might mean. He looks, she thinks, just like an empty can of gasoline—a shell containing both exhaustion and a volatile rage. She envies him and his certainty. He seems to know his life's path from its poor beginning to its end.

There is a question that she has been asking herself for weeks now, without ever coming closer to an answer or to knowing why it seems so important. Whether being home has magnified her own unhappiness or if it has simply brought her mind the clarity it needed to compose an answer doesn't matter. She feels better once she has decided that she hopes her child will be a boy.

From the kitchen window, Hem sees Kate and Lorraine painting stars and rockets on the barn while Trevor gives directions.

He's happy to see Trevor on his feet again and happy to have Kate back home. She looks older, softer, and tired, but he likes to think that, now she has come home, he has a second chance to steer her right. He's a little disappointed that she has spent all day outside, hanging lights on poles that he has hammered in the yard, cleaning up old, rusted lawn games, and setting up old buckets for iced drinks. All while he remains indoors, baking cakes and drinking tea.

For the first time in a long time, he looks seriously at his wife's face and notices an unfamiliar weariness. There are signs of worry and hard use—cracking skin and clouded eyes—but also of subdued acceptance. Hem sees that, at some point in the years since they left Providence, after years of unpaid bills and poor living, with their little savings draining away, she has given up hope that things will ever be much better. At some point, she decided that she had no other choice—that this was all she could expect of life. At some point, this consummate change occurred, and he, in his amazing selfishness, just missed it.

But the front door opens, its hinges screeching. He turns to find Lorraine behind him, leaning on the jamb between the kitchen and the hall. She looks at him with wonder, excitement, and despair.

"She's pregnant."

He's quiet, eyes slanted uncertainly towards the floor. Lorraine coughs and pushes past him to the sink, where she grabs the soap and washes her hands gently, making hardly any noise.

"I promised her I wouldn't tell you. She's upset enough. She doesn't need another argument, especially with you."

She dries her hands and comes to put them on his face and neck. She says, "Try to be happy."

"Are you?"

She shrugs. "What else would I be?"

He's clouded, numb. Outside the kitchen window, he can see Kate rolling in the grass, her brother clutched in her arms. She won't let him go, though he struggles hard against her, blindly, like a fish.

"It doesn't matter," he says.

Lorraine sighs, laughs, and leaves the house, and Hem is left alone with his infuriating thoughts.

Later, as he puts the chicken in the oven and considers opening a bottle of wine, the phone rings. It is Mrs. Russell telling him that they won't be able to attend the party. Hem tells her that he hopes everything is all right, but doesn't think much about it until half an hour and a dozen phone calls later when he realizes that the party has effectively been canceled.

When his family comes in from the yard, they are all smiling and making noise as they remove their muddy shoes and help a beaming Trevor kick his way upstairs. To Hem, they seem as happy as they ever have, as he remembers them before Kate moved out and before Trevor broke his leg. He likes to think that this is almost how they were in Providence before the move.

Tonight, he will have to listen to his daughter talk as though he doesn't know. He's frightened of the dreams that he knows he will have: of grandchildren with pale, thin faces, blue-veined fingers, and dull, black eyes. Children all born certain that the world is as dark and tangled and as full of clatter as the dying useless tunnels of the goddamned Federal Mine.

CHAPTER 36

GEORGE

The barn breathes the way it always has—deep and damp, with pockets of ammonia in the corners and the slow rise of dust when the door slides open. George steps inside, letting the light catch up. It flickers once, then holds.

Eustace is alive and standing, though he has one thick black shoulder pressed against the stall rail. George touches his side, just to feel the warmth. He sits down on the feed bucket, letting the wood groan beneath him. The bull flicks its ear and breathes out. There's no other sound.

Lately, he's been thinking about legacy. He once thought that his would be a son. Some squat, hard-headed boy with dirt on his shins and something like purpose in his jaw. There had been a time when he believed it was coming. That twenty-three-year-old summer. The girl with the stutter and the sad little birthmark just under her clavicle. George mailed cash to a PO box until the envelopes started coming back unopened. He still dreams of a boy some nights—brown-eyed, turning away.

Mica came a while after, from a different girl and a

different kind of vanishing. No car. No note. Just George, left all alone with a responsibility he couldn't manage. When she was three, she used to squint at him like he'd gotten her name wrong. She asked once if her mother loved her. George didn't think. He just said yes.

Still. Still, there are nights like this one. Barn cool, and the bull sleeping. And something in him—an ache he doesn't try to name. Not regret, exactly. Just the outline of something missing. The kind of missing that has a temperature.

The guilt comes softly, like the weight of fog on the fields. He doesn't blame her. It isn't about blame. It's about how some things just don't pass down right. How the shapes you hold inside your head all melt as soon as someone else picks them up.

He thinks of what he could have passed down. His slow temper. The way he folds his maps. But Mica didn't get those things. She didn't need them. He could raise her softer.

Still.

He places a hand against the bull's side. Listens to the ribs moving underneath.

"You're doing good," he says. "You're all right."

A bird rustles above, maybe a dove, maybe not. He doesn't look.

Outside, the air is darker than it should be. He waits for a sound that doesn't come, and then he leaves, stepping quiet, like something's watching. Like something always has been.

CHAPTER 37

KATE

The hood lamp over the stove casts long shadows onto the linoleum. Kate stands barefoot by the sink, mug in hand, the tea inside it long gone cold. The window's black glass offers back her shape, doubled—her shoulders slightly tilted, her hair caught in a twist behind her ear. Outside, the wind presses gently against the house, touching the windows but never insisting.

The house smells faintly of boiled potatoes. She doesn't remember what they had for dinner. Or if they ate together. The silence has grown its own spine, stretching between rooms.

She presses the rim of the mug against her lip but doesn't drink.

Behind her, the floor creaks. Just once. Deliberate. Not curious, not sneaking. Then the long pause. Lorraine steps through the doorway. "Are you still thinking about leaving?"

Kate doesn't turn around. "I don't know what I'm thinking."

Lorraine waits. Then she says, "Your father—he wasn't always like this."

"You've told me."

"No. I mean, he really wasn't. There were nights he'd drive out to meet me with a blanket and a thermos, and we'd sit in the back of the car and listen to rain. He used to draw maps on my arm with his finger. Said he was tracing all the roads we'd take."

Kate turns, leans against the counter. "What happened?"

"Nothing big. Just one day, the blanket stayed in the trunk. The maps stopped being drawn. And I kept thinking they'd come back."

Kate studies her mother's face. "Did you ever wish you'd left?"

Lorraine shrugs. "Some days. But most days I just wish I'd asked him why he stopped."

Kate says nothing. The sink drips once, then again.

"It's not always about choosing the right person," Lorraine adds. "Sometimes it's just about choosing. And then choosing again. Every day."

Kate nods, once, sharply. She doesn't trust her voice.

Lorraine steps away. "If you go, just make sure you're still drawing maps."

Kate stays at the sink, staring at the spot where the steam has faded from the metal basin.

Chapter 38

Mountain

There is a pot of fried spaghetti on the stove. His father curses when he finds it cold. He cuts it in two with his belt knife and drops each half onto a plate, then heats them in the microwave. As Mason sits to eat, Spoon asks him if he's still seeing Lily.

"Yes, sir."

"Found out she's a Pearson. They're charity cases. Trash, you know." He shakes his head. "I don't mean leave it all alone. Just take it slow, and don't hold onto her too long."

Mason nods. Spoon grunts and wanders off into the den. Mason hears the phone click off its cradle, followed by the muffled sound of his father's voice.

The two plates of spaghetti steam. Mason's mother is down in the basement, sleeping off a bad day. Mason stabs his fork into his plate, but can't eat. It seems to him that all his life, at home, he has been listening to muffled voices. Not so long ago, he would have seen things in the steam from this spaghetti, like animals and human faces. He would have seen dances in the air between his father's plate and his thermal cavitations that would slowly cool back into clean, invisible air. In many ways, he's unhappy to find that his world is much bigger now. He can see the mess his parents have made of their kitchen—splattered oil on the wall above the stove, burnt strips of paper on the walls, the cracked refrigerator door, the patchwork of missing linoleum—he has not thought about any of these things until now when he wonders how they must look to his school friends, who all live in the neat little houses in the valley. He imagines that the people in those houses always sit together, all in one room, and look straight at one another as much as they please.

In the den, his father's voice softens, as though he's trying to smooth something over, which means he's almost done. The spaghetti has cooled, and Mason is afraid to touch it, knowing it will come up in a single mass, impossible to pick apart.

CHAPTER 39

VALLEY

After dinner, Hem, Kate, and Lorraine drink wine together on the porch while Trevor, who should be asleep, gets ready for the day ahead. They can hear the whispers of his cast scraping on the floor above them.

The night air pulses with the sound of insects, and the ground is covered with a coarse gray mist. Hem has not yet said a word about the phone calls. He has tried to catch Lorraine's eye, hoping she will ask him what is wrong. Now, he knows that he's running out of time.

He says, "This afternoon, while you were both out in the yard—"

Kate is sitting on the porch steps, arms around her knees.

"They all called. Everybody canceled."

"What?" Lorraine says. "Who?"

"Everyone. I spent an hour taking calls."

They stare down at the back of Kate's neck, which is moon-white, pockmarked with a line of blackfly bites.

Hem says, "I didn't want to tell you around Trevor."

"That makes no sense," says Lorraine. "There has to be a reason."

"We can't tell him." Kate does not turn, only leans to rest her chin upon her knees. Her head is swallowed up by darkness.

"Well," Lorraine says. She's moving to get up and go inside, though she moves slowly, and she keeps her eyes on Hem. "There must be a good reason, even if they aren't telling us. It's rude, and I'm angry, but there's plenty of summer left. We'll just move it to next weekend."

"It's Trevor," Hem says.

Kate says, "He can't handle it. Not now."

Hem stares out at the lawn. There is no moon, and fireflies appear like falling stars. He feels as though his organs have been long in disarray and now sighs suddenly back into place.

Lorraine says, "Let's go feed the cats."

Kate stands and stretches with her, both their faces twisting in the porch light.

They are halfway to the barn when the phone rings. Lorraine's voice floats out of the darkness. "If they're calling to cancel, tell them they can fuck off."

Kate laughs, but without much force.

The ringing stops before Hem opens the front door. He finds Trevor in the living room, holding the receiver.

"You should be in bed," Hem says. "Here, let me."

Trevor hands him the phone. "I can't find tape for my fins."

"We'll find some after this. Wait for me upstairs, okay?"

He waits, holding the phone pressed hard against his chest until he hears Trevor's door shut. In his mind, he sees Kate walking to the barn. She used to walk with her hands balled up in her pockets, kicking her legs straight ahead of her with every step. Now, she sets her feet down carefully, as though she has become aware of and afraid of her fragility.

"Hem?" the voice says, breathless, like it had been running.

"Speaking. Who is this?"

"Spoon. Sullivan. We haven't really met. Not proper, anyway. But I know who you are. I think you know who I am, too."

Hem glances at the clock. "Yeah, I guess. It's late."

There's a pause on the line. A wheeze, maybe. Or a laugh. "Yeah, that's what they keep telling me. It's late. It's always late, isn't it?"

Hem frowns, towel now clutched against his chest. "Can I help you with something?"

"Yeah," Spoon says. "Yeah. I'm calling to invite you to a birthday party."

"A party?"

"For Trevor."

Hem stiffens. "Why would you be throwing a party for my son?"

"Because he's a good kid. And because you let him keep Sonny. I figure that deserves something. You like cake, Hem?"

The line goes quiet for a second too long. Hem hears static, or breathing, or both.

"Look," Spoon continues, words slurring slightly, "We've got a spot out here—real nice. I've got a table under the trees. Lanterns. I'm thinking—cake, a couple candles, maybe some music. Kids love that."

Hem doesn't answer. The voice on the other end is too cheerful, too smooth. Something about it rubs wrong. There's an edge in it—hollow and stretched, like a string pulled too tight.

"You still there?"

"I'm here," Hem says. "I just don't understand."

"Nothing to understand. Just goodwill. Just people trying to be neighborly. That's what this place needs, right? Neighbors who know each other."

Hem glances out the window, where the dark presses hard against the glass.

"I appreciate the offer," he says, slow and careful. "But I think we'll keep things quiet this year."

Another silence. Then: "That's fine. No hard feelings. Just —don't be surprised if he gets a gift anyway. I've got something in mind."

Hem's hand tightens around the receiver. "What kind of gift?"

But the line clicks and goes dead.

He stares at the phone in his hand for a long time, thinking of Kate and Lorraine on their way back from the barn. Neither one speaks, though their hands swing gently at their sides, long white fingers sometimes touching, joining with and parting from each other effortlessly.

CHAPTER 40

MARCH

He comes in late, which is the only way he knows how. The doors are open and the air smells like lighter fluid and damp wood, and something sour behind that. No one turns to look, but he imagines they've already seen him.

It's not clear whose party it is. There's a banner hung crooked across the back wall that says "Happy Birthday, George" though George has been sick or missing or dead for some time now. Someone else's idea, probably. Maybe Spoon's.

March finds a seat at a folding table near the bleachers, low light pushing dust down through the rafters. Cal is there, and Vincent, both of them old in different ways. Cal with a fish-hook in his hatband, Vincent with a paper wristband he's been too lazy or too proud to cut off. Neither of them looks up when March sits. "It's the same crowd as always," Cal says eventually.

Vincent laughs into his drink. "Except more of them. And louder."

Across the room, Spoon is surrounded by the new boys—

shirt collars limp, boots too clean. One has a tablet tucked under his arm. Another holds a clipboard like he's afraid of it. Spoon says something. The boys laugh.

March watches the gesture—how Spoon leans in, how the others lean out. His voice lifts above the others for a second, then drops back into static.

"You hear about the thing in Mania?" Cal says.

"Which thing?"

"Something went wrong in Mania," Vincent says. "Heard they sent three trucks instead of two."

"That's all?" Cal asks.

"Someone brought a badge," Vincent says, and lets it sit there.

March scratches at the condensation on his can. "So what?"

"So nothing," says Cal. "Just that it's happening again."

March sips his drink. It tastes like aluminum and regret. "No."

Vincent leans in, suddenly too close. "Lot of boys are working double shifts now. Lot of new ones. Young ones."

Cal nods. "Too young."

They all look over at Spoon. He's laughing now, but it looks like it hurts. There's a flash behind his eyes that says he's counting exits. The clipboard guy pats him on the back and whispers something.

They're quiet. The speaker above them crackles, then plays a song too slow for movement. A woman in boots tries to sway to it, loses rhythm, retreats.

"You think he's in trouble?" March asks.

Vincent shakes his head. "Spoon's never in trouble. He's the reason trouble exists."

Cal stares down into his can. "That was true once."

The music changes. Someone's put on a song too slow for

the energy in the room. A few people sway uncertainly, then give up.

March says, "I don't think I was invited."

"You weren't," says Cal. "But that's never mattered much."

From the corner, Spoon catches March's eye. Just for a second. Enough to nod, or grimace, or both. March doesn't nod back.

The lights dim for no reason. Someone drops a plate. A dog barks outside.

Vincent whispers, "You know, I saw him yelling at one of the new ones last week. In the back lot. Had him by the collar like a schoolboy."

"Maybe he deserved it."

"Maybe Spoon needed to feel like he could still hold someone by the collar."

Cal says nothing. Just takes another sip, and watches the wall like it might move.

From here, the bunting looks like old laundry strung between poles. The light overhead twitches and settles. March smells something burnt. Maybe the steak. Maybe the wiring.

"Still," Vincent mutters, "He's not wrong, about most things."

"No," Cal says. "He just isn't always right anymore."

Outside, a dog starts barking and doesn't stop. No one goes to shut it up.

March leans back. He lets the noise fold around him, the tinny chorus of metal chairs, the off-beat clink of cans. For a moment, he thinks he hears someone saying his name. He closes his eyes. Feels the chair under him. The sweat at the base of his neck. The low thrum of the lights. He tells himself it's nothing.

That it always was.

CHAPTER 41

KATE

Kate sits on the edge of the truck bed with her legs swinging slowly over the bumper. The metal is warm, almost sticky, even though it's nearing midnight. Across the gravel drive, Connor's friends are passing around something in a sweating bottle. Their voices are high and loose. Every laugh is a little too loud.

Sam is halfway through a story about a fight he saw down at the mill—some guy from Cavalcade had his jaw dislocated with a pipe. Jack is jabbing at the fire with a tire iron, saying he could've taken both guys easy. Connor leans against the tailgate, his arm lightly pressed against hers.

He hasn't said much either, just watched his friends with that half-lidded ease that Kate has come to associate with resignation. Not boredom, exactly—just the sense that everything is what it is.

"They're harmless," he says to her when she glances sideways. "Mostly."

She smiles, but only a little. "They work with your dad?"

"Some of them. Others just hang around."

She watches the firelight flicker across their faces, trying to memorize the way they look: young and loud and already worn thin around the edges. Like they know something she doesn't..

When Spoon's name comes up—Nick is joking about the "birthday invitation" Spoon tried to send to some kid, laughing like it's the most absurd thing in the world—Kate stiffens. Connor notices.

"I told him not to," he says quietly. "He gets ideas."

Kate nods, her voice low. "People are saying the cops are circling. That someone's going to pay for what happened with those dogs."

Connor doesn't answer right away. He pulls a splinter from the truck bed and tosses it towards the fire.

"They're always circling," he says finally. "They'd rather have a reason to lock him up, but for now he's got too much pull. Seriously, it would take something over-the-top. More than a hurt dog, anyway."

She studies him in profile. In the firelight, he looks older. Harder. Not like the boy from the quarry with the stupid moon joke.

These nights with his friends—bare bulbs strung through branches, music crackling through a radio, stories retold so often they've hardened into legend—have a rhythm she's starting to recognize. It's not friendship, exactly. More like shared inertia.

She wonders where else she'd go. She thinks about school, but it's blurry. About Providence, but it's distant. Here, at least, there's a place to sit. A hand resting just against hers.

Mick shouts for Connor to come help him find another bottle, and Connor jumps down from the tailgate.

Kate stays where she is, legs swinging in the dark, watching shadows leap and scatter like startled deer. In a town like this, she thinks, you don't get to belong by choosing. You belong by staying. And sometimes that's the only choice that feels real.

CHAPTER 42

MOUNTAIN

Spoon is self-aware enough to know that he is on a bender, and one worse than any of the dozens he can easily recall. He knows from past experience that it will not end well. The way that it takes hold of him is like the quiet infiltration of a virus, giving no appreciable sign until it is already much too late for him to check its course. He can only hope that it will end soon and won't leave too much lasting damage.

After he hangs up the phone, he goes immediately to the kitchen table, where his whiskey bottle sits. For a moment, he enjoys just holding it securely in his hands, believing that it does exactly what he asks of it. Then he pours himself a glass and drinks it, and as soon as he can feel the burning in his belly, he can feel his mind returning. He decides another glass won't hurt, so he pours and drinks this, too.

He goes into the next room, where there is a television, a couch, and a trunk of drugs that he can only keep away from for as long as it takes to decide, once more, that he deserves them.

CHAPTER 43

VALLEY

At first, moving out of Providence seemed like fate. If Hem had been a religious man, he would have certainly seen God's hand at work. There was a freshness in the air—a snap and tickle that he couldn't stop admiring. They were, he thought, so far ahead of any problem he'd created that the bad times had no chance of catching up. There was a magic there in Shokten—something old and powerful. He had been waiting for it—wanting it—for so long. And he had it now. This feeling that the things he'd imagined would be revealed. That everything would be okay.

The dogs—they haunted him—despite his feeling that they were much better off. It wasn't as if he'd tried to hide it. He'd reported everyone. The truth is, he got lazy. If there is anything that still pains him after all this time, it's this—that he had no better excuse. After watching strays come in, go out, and come again, he simply got annoyed and took an easier route. For most of them, he'd only sped up an inevitable fate.

But there were some who didn't feel the same as he did and who cared enough to read public records. When they tried to stop him, they discovered the drinking. It was this, more than anything else, that lost him his home and his practice—as Lorraine always told him it would. It didn't matter, as he always thought it would, that he finally quit. By then, it seemed the damage was done.

Lorraine didn't judge him then as harshly as he might have expected. She seemed more relieved that he'd given it up. But he sometimes wonders if the resentment she should have felt back then has finally begun to build. What if she had only saved it up, stored it away like wine, to age? He sees her watching him from a dark upstairs window and realizes she doesn't care that he is leaving.

The day they left Providence was the strangest day of her life. It wouldn't necessarily have been if they had been moving somewhere more familiar, if they'd planned, or if she'd had family in the town to visit. But her parents died soon after Kate was born, and Hem had never had much family to speak of. He never really had what she would call relationships at all.

Years ago, she wished like hell her dad was still alive—when Trevor was just starting to become a person, following his father everywhere, picking up his mannerisms and the patterns of his speech, his words—his thoughts. She was jealous, maybe, and a little defensive. She didn't like that Trevor only had one spring to drink from.

And at that time, Hem was such a deep and poisoned spring. He'd put all of his pain on the world, building it into the awful place that he'd discovered it to be. She never cared about the dogs—she knew enough to know the world isn't perfect and agreed that they were better off dead. And she didn't care about the license. But they'd had options. It wouldn't have been too hard to stay.

The day they left, Hem and Trevor woke up early to finish packing the car. They gave the thing an air of celebration, slapping palms and calling it the "Big Change." Trevor was too young to have too much to lose. Of course, neither did Hem.

He had always dreamed of getting out of Providence. "Stepping out," he called it.

Meanwhile, she and Kate had friends. However, it didn't take long to lose touch. And things that, though, as Hem put it, were more human fascination than reality, seemed real enough to them. Things like going to restaurants, shopping, Kate's soccer team. And she remembers thinking, there is no good reason why that shouldn't be enough. Regardless of his own beliefs, she thinks his family has to matter. It should matter in a way that nothing else does.

As they left the leafy, old New England streets of Providence and passed into the mountains, she was constantly thinking of how she had let Hem convince her. She supposes, in the end, it came down to her stupid, blind trust in his dreams. She'd been much younger then—ten years is still a long stretch when it's placed between thirty and 40—and she'd spent so much time up till then believing—no, knowing—that Hem was the smarter half—the one who it made sense to follow. She supposes that at that time, Kate thought the same way about her.

The first thing that she noticed was a "lifting," something like a glass jar rising from a fly. She looked out at the blue land, the mountains disappearing into the mist, and admitted that what Hem had said was right: she felt free. Or at least much less restricted. It seemed, in this place—this strange, wild place—it wouldn't matter what she wore or how she acted—what she read into a friend's sly smile as she caught it between the poetry and self-help sections of the library.

For an hour or so, she was able to believe that Hem was right—that clean slates were much better than attempts at fixing what went wrong. A solid hour, during which she tried so hard to put things in perspective, to believe that lately, they'd become blurred.

It was the moment they "stepped out"—truly stepped out

—that snapped her back. The mountains faded in the background. That she had expected. But what opened up ahead of them wasn't at all what she'd imagined (and she'd tried hard to imagine right). It was, she thinks, like it must be for prisoners to see a prison.

And then, of course, there was the fact that she enjoyed the glass jar. In it, she had been no prisoner, as the trees, the mountains, and the smooth roads made her feel. It was a safety net. A boundary firmly planted, between herself and want—herself and true pain. She did not remember how Hem got her to agree.

"Hem, can we stop a minute?" she remembers saying.

"Really? It's only been a couple of hours."

"Kate and I need a bathroom."

Kate pulled out her headphones and looked over at her. "I'm fine."

"But you'd rather stop, right? We have time."

"That's true," Hem says. "The house has been there fifty years. It isn't falling down today."

And that's when she believed, for just a minute, that he'd planned this. Not just since he lost his license, but before—back when he found her, working as a hostess at the Providence Inn.

She said, "I don't think we know what we're doing here."

"Lorraine, we said we'd try it. If it doesn't work out, we'll move back."

"And how will we know when it hasn't worked? Just wait until the kids are old enough to tell us?"

Hem said, "That's life."

She would bring all of this up again, but doesn't think he would remember.

CHAPTER 44

MOUNTAIN

Hem's first impression of Spoon's place is that it looks more like a camp than a home. The moonlight, glancing off the mist in the valley below, reveals a plateau spider-webbed with sunken pathways leading to decrepit buildings that slowly sag in the mud.

The road leads to the main house, which is large but simply built, a square two-story, like a castle, without wings or a porch.

As soon as he shuts off his lights and engine, he's greeted by a hard knock on the windshield. He inhales and ducks his head. The look he sees on Spoon's face now is not so different from the one on Trevor's as he waited for the doctor to re-break his leg.

Hem grabs his bag and steps out, locking the door behind him.

"That all?" Spoon says.

"All what?"

"The bag. That everything?"

"It's all I have."

Spoon looks off into the distance as if he's thinking of a

way to change this. "Alright then," he says. "The kennel's back here."

On this hill, the sound of summer insects isn't as invasive as it seems down in the valley. There are only murmurs, like the lapping of a calm sea.

Spoon unlocks a chain looped through the handles of the kennel doors.

"I got the sick one up front."

Hem squints against the scraping sound of brittle claws. A single bulb burns in the kennel, shedding insufficient light upon an aisle flanked by rows of narrow cages. In the first, a boy about Trevor's age is squatting by a pregnant bitch.

"All right," Spoon says. "Come out now."

"Nothing's changed," the boy says. He is shoeless, wearing only sweatpants and a bleach-stained shirt. His eyes are caked with rheum.

"That's good."

"Yeah, except she's coughing now."

When the boy steps out into the light, Hem sees his face is squashed and ugly. He can't tell why.

Spoon turns away and rubs his head. "She's the one," he says. "Supposed to be a pharaoh hound. You know what that is?"

Hem nods. He can see the dog is thin despite her bloated belly. She's short-haired, small, with red ears, wide as trowels.

"Expensive," Hem says. "Hope she's worth it."

Spoon sniffs. "Will be. People up in Providence pay anything."

Hem goes into the cage, opens up his bag, and finds his stethoscope. The dog's heart sounds fine, but her breath is rattling. At his touch, she lifts her head and runs her nose along his arm.

"How old is she?" he asks.

"Five years," says Spoon.

Hem tilts her head and looks into her eyes. The balls are coated with a bluish film. He doesn't know if the worms now writhing in his belly were born of fear or anger.

"I'd guess that she's a few years older."

"No one asked," Spoon says. He starts to pace along the run. "I need this litter out of her. All right? That's it."

"Well, listen to me, then."

The boy stands near the door, not shuffling his feet or fiddling but standing still and quiet, staring out into the night. Spoon's boots make squelching sounds as he walks up and down the aisle.

The dog has an infection. Hem knows he can cure it, though he wonders. She's not afraid of death and will not mind oblivion. But he can't deny that he does not know what will happen to the puppies. He can't imagine them—not suffering, not there, alone, and in the dark.

"What's the word?" Spoon stomps back up the run. "You need more time?"

Hem finds a bottle of Doxycycline and steps out of the cage. Spoon walks outside and motions for Hem to follow.

In the moonlight, in the night-hum, Hem can see that Spoon's anxiety has been replaced by anger.

"I'll be straight with you," Spoon says. "You'd better fix that dog."

Hem holds the bottle out, flat, on an empty palm.

"She's got a bad infection. Give her two a day, with food."

Spoon rubs his head. "Won't hurt the litter?"

"They'll be fine. But you should feed her. She's too thin."

"That dog's made for hunting, you know? She'll turn just like a—like an antelope. Just cut right off—just like a fucking antelope inside a goddamn thicket."

Hem nods. He's trying to imagine Spoon's face when he finds out that the dog is just a mutt. But for once, he seems unable to get much outside himself.

"You listen," Spoon says. "They'll be good dogs. Not just good. Important."

"If you say so, but she needs food."

Spoon looks past Hem back into the kennel.

"You'll stay with her."

"What?"

"You'll stay."

"I can't stay here," Hem says. "I have to go home."

Spoon's response is a firm shove. Before Hem realizes what is happening, he's back inside the kennel, watching as the doors swing shut behind him.

Hem steps back into the aisle. It takes him a minute, standing in the blue light, to decide that Spoon is really not returning. When he does, he is surprised by his composure. He believes that if he keeps the dog alive until morning, Spoon will come back mostly sober, and Hem will go straight to the police. To orient himself, he walks slowly down the length of the run—fifty feet or so of concrete and steel mesh. Black eyes watch him from the semi-darkness, but the dogs all stay unnaturally silent. At the end of the run is an open window, through which he can see the moon and stars, as well as the peninsula, spread out beneath him like the broad back of a whale, strewn with yellow lights of houses and the thick black scabs of wooded hills. He hopes that when Lorraine wakes, she will not panic. His throat tightens with a sudden thirst.

He goes back along the run, through the now familiar smells of feed and bleach and urine, to the open door of the cage. In the dim light, he sees Mason slugged into his corner, head between his knees.

"Is there someplace to get a drink in here?" Hem says. "A hose or something?"

Mason lifts his head and points. In an alcove near the door, Hem finds a spigot and a filthy length of rubber hose. He lets the water run for a while and then laps at the stream until his mouth feels clean again. When he closes the spigot, Mason's timid voice calls out to him: "If you drink too much, you'll have to pee."

Hem sits down against the wall by the dog's head and comforts himself with the soft spot just behind her big ears.

"Will your dad let us out?"

Mason shakes his head and turns back to the wall.

"In the morning. Maybe lunchtime, yeah."

"Does he do this often?"

Mason shrugs.

The dog begins to cough, and Hem moves his hand to her chest to calm her. He thinks maybe later, he will give her a second dose. He's ashamed to admit that he wants Spoon to be pleased with her progress.

Mason scratches at his inner thigh. At first, it's absent-minded, but as he continues, his administrations grow increasingly violent.

"What is it?" Hem says. "What's wrong?"

Mason stops and stares.

"What's wrong with your leg?"

"Nothing."

"You keep scratching at it."

"It's a spider bite. Sometimes I get allergic."

"Where's your mother?"

For a moment, Mason stares at him with fire in his eyes. Then he turns aside. Hem opens up his bag and searches for a bottle of neem oil.

"Here, this will help."

"That's for animals," says Mason, and refuses to take it.

Reason is a petty thing. But even in the darkness, there are differences of degree.

"Listen," Hem says, dropping the bottle back into his bag, "I'm too old to sleep on the ground. How do we get out of here?"

Mason blinks, his face disturbingly pale in the moonlight. "We just have to wait."

"You don't know any other way out?"

He walks over to the window. It is not locked but is very old and appears to be painted shut.

"Have you ever tried the window?"

"No, sir," says Mason.

Hem begins to understand. "You can't reach it."

"No. There's nothing to stand on."

Hem is already in motion, stalking back towards the front of the kennel, bringing all the dogs to attention.

"Come here," he says. "Help me move one of these barrels."

Mason isn't much help, but together, they manage to scrape one of the large barrels along the run and position it under the pane.

Hem climbs up and tries the window with both hands. It doesn't move. Near the bottom, he can see a ridge where paint has pooled up over time.

"It's stuck," he says. "I need something to pick this paint off with."

Mason is quiet. Hem wonders if he even wants to break out.

"Go get my bag," he says.

At the very bottom, he finds an old, blunted scalpel and goes to work on the paint, chipping away both it and the wood beneath it in small chunks.

Mason stands quietly at his side, watching.

Hem says, "Don't worry. You don't have to leave if you don't want to."

Mason shrugs. "I don't mind."

Hem is halfway through. He can already feel the window frame begin to loosen.

"Bullshit," he says. "It's cold, and it smells like dog food."

Mason laughs. It's choked a little, like he's tried to keep it in, and comes out strangely high-pitched.

Hem grins. "To be honest, I don't think your dad will know the difference."

Mason says, "Probably not."

Hem puts down the scalpel and raises the pane. It resists him but rises in fits and starts until the frame is clear.

"All right," he says. "Let's get you through first."

Mason lets Hem lift him up onto the barrel, where he wastes no time worming through the hole.

"I'm afraid I'll land on my head," he says.

"Make sure you hold onto the frame. You have to do a kind of somersault."

"Ow!" Mason cries out, falling to the ground. Hem puts his head up through the window.

"Are you all right?"

Mason is lying on his side, holding his hand and rocking back and forth.

"I think I cut myself."

Hem feels along the base of the window frame and finds a small nail sticking through the wood.

"How bad is it?"

"I can't tell."

"Can you stand up? Let me see."

Mason takes a breath and gets onto his feet. He has torn his hand diagonally, from thumb to little finger.

Hem searches through his bag and finds some bandages.

"Here."

He wants to show Mason how to use them, but when he tries to squeeze his own body through the hole, his shoulders stop him.

"Damn it," he says. "Look, I'll have to tell you how, okay?"

Mason has the bandage unwrapped and has already begun to apply it.

Hem says, "That's good. Don't let it get too tight."

When Mason finishes, he reaches up to hand the unused bandages back through the window.

"That's all right. You keep them. But watch the bleeding. If it doesn't stop soon, you should wake your mother up."

Mason says, "Thank you," and nods. He makes his exit quickly, without fuss.

For some reason, he can't explain, Hem moves the barrel back to its place near the door. He sits down on top of it, focusing for a moment on the sounds of leaves outside moving in the breeze. Then he hears a whine and looks down at the bitch he'd come this far to see.

Hem sighs. "You never wanted puppies, did you?"

She stares at him with milky eyes, neither pleased nor displeased by his presence.

CHAPTER 45

VALLEY

Lorraine and Trevor sit at the edge of the creek, their shoes off, feet dipped into the slow-moving water. The evening is warm and still. Fireflies hang in the heavy air like punctuation. Trevor balances a flat rock on his knee, staring down at his reflection.

"Did Dad used to be different?" he asks.

Lorraine pulls her feet from the water, tucks them beneath her on the rock. "What makes you ask that?"

Trevor shrugs. "He doesn't smile like he used to. And he forgets stuff. And sometimes it's like he's not even there."

Lorraine looks up at the trees, watches a bird dart through the last light. "He's tired, Trev. Not just in his body, but in his head. That happens to people sometimes."

"Did he used to be fun? Like... ever?"

"Once," she says. "He told jokes. Made pancakes in weird shapes. Sang out of tune just to make us laugh."

"What happened?"

She thinks about how to explain it, how to shape the truth into something a child can carry.

"He tried hard for a long time. Tried to make everything

work. But sometimes, when things keep falling apart no matter how hard you try, a person starts to give up. Just a little, at first. Then more."

Trevor nods slowly. He pushes the rock into the water and watches it sink.

"Is he mad at me?"

"No," Lorraine says. "He loves you. Even when it doesn't seem like it. He just doesn't always know how to show it."

"Will he get better?"

She hesitates. "I don't know. But you and me—we're okay. We can still be okay."

He leans against her side, his shoulder fitting neatly under her arm.

"You miss him?" he asks.

"I miss the part of him that used to tell jokes," she says. "But I'm still here. And so are you. And that's something."

They sit that way until the last light drains from the sky, the hush of the creek and the chirp of crickets folding around them like a blanket.

Chapter 46

Kennel

In Hem's dreams, he is often taller than he is in life.

Tonight, he towers over an immense field. It is wheat, or corn, or rice. It stretches far away from him, towards mud-capped mountains in the distance.

His whole family is around him, staring up at him expectantly, and he's very hungry. It is like no hunger he has ever felt —not stomach pain or weakness, but— a fog—a mental haze he knows will only dissipate once he has eaten. His mind works fitfully, in brief and concentrated bursts, working problems he can't be sure exist.

Lorraine holds out a small bowl covered with a white cloth. He's so tall that he must bend to reach it.

There is no cloth. Eyes—all eight of them—are glistening. Are shining in the bowl's curve. In its light.

The spider is gigantic, lying at the bottom of the bowl, its legs bent underneath it.

Hem doesn't move. He believes in—he trusts in—the spider. He knows what it is to spin, to weave. He knows what it is like to live in trap and home.

He reaches down into the bowl and cups the spider in the hollow of his hand. Its hairs are stiff and sticky.

It keeps its body still, but Hem feels movement underneath. Its hairy mandibles begin to lift, revealing two red fangs that slowly stretch out—stretching out—above his wrist.

His mind works quickly but erratically. Like a drugged detective, building out a web of tenuous connections that appear to justify the sum of all existence.

The spider's fangs leave small red spots behind them on his pale skin. Now its spinnerets begin to work, and it releases silk in golden spurts, binding all his fingers tightly.

Lorraine is smiling, and Kate stares off across the field. Hem is scared of being lost inside the spool. It will envelop him. He will be lost for days, months, years, until, emerging, he will find himself a different being, tall and trembling, groping its way through a vast, kaleidoscopic world.

Only on the rarest of occasions, when the spinning seems done, will he look up from his work and find it is no different from the work of others of his kind who, in their quest for order, have all spun the same web, and been jealous, and descended into chaos once again.

Anger and aggression are not twins but distant cousins, with a thousand children who all speak and act in ways that are so similar it takes a careful study to describe their differences.

CHAPTER 47

LORRAINE

It's evening, and the sun has folded itself halfway behind the hills, the way it does in this part of the valley—slow at first, then suddenly gone. Lorraine sits on the porch steps with a dish towel still slung over one shoulder.

Kate is barefoot in the grass, a tennis ball in one hand, eyes narrowed. Across from her, Trevor crouches like a runner, his face tilted upward, his shirt hanging off one shoulder. She tosses it high. He lunges. Misses. The ball rolls towards the barn. They both laugh.

Lorraine watches them with her hands resting loosely on her knees. She doesn't call out. Doesn't interrupt. She knows the rules of this game. It's the one where the goal is only to move—back and forth, again and again—without keeping score, without letting the air go still. Something unspoken gets passed between them, even when the ball doesn't. She can't remember the last time they played like this. Maybe before Trevor started speaking in half-thoughts. Before Kate grew into that cool quiet she wears like a coat.

The lawn is uneven. The ball bounces oddly. Trevor chases

it, shrieking, and Kate bends over laughing. The sound startles a crow from the cedar, and it lifts off into the pink sky.

Lorraine shifts on the step. Her thighs stick to the wood.

The air smells like dandelion stems and ash. She lights a cigarette, though it tastes sour and flaked. She doesn't care. She wants the smell to settle into her shirt, her hair. She wants to be able to catch a trace of it later, when the game's long done and the porch is empty again.

Kate throws the ball underhand this time. Trevor catches it and throws it back too hard. She ducks. The ball hits the siding behind her and drops. They stare at each other, both smiling, but something in their posture has shifted. The game's unraveling.

Lorraine exhales smoke through her nose. She leans back on her hands and watches the light leave the grass. There's still just enough to see the scuff marks on Kate's knees, the way Trevor's hands hang loose at his sides.

Soon it'll be too dark to keep going.

Soon someone will say it.

Kate kicks the ball gently with the side of her foot. "Last one?"

Trevor nods.

The ball rises, arcs, falls.

It's not caught.

They both watch it land and roll away.

Lorraine flicks the ash and waits.

CHAPTER 48

KENNEL

The night gives way to morning grudgingly, turning the light inside the kennel from the murky purple of a bruise to gun-barrel blue and finally to a uniform shade of gray. Hem wakes to the racket of the chain in the door handles and to the dog's suddenly alert and watchful eyes.

Spoon enters with his head hung low as if in thought. It is obvious he has not been to sleep. He looks exhausted and cowed, which makes Hem think whatever drug had shot his pupils out the night before has mostly worn off.

Spoon holds a mug of instant coffee, which he offers to Hem. It is lukewarm, much too strong, and coated with a foam of crystallized grounds.

Hem expects something—a threat or an apology—but Spoon seems more concerned with his dog. Stepping into the cage, he says hoarsely, "She looks better."

"I gave her a shot. She still needs those pills, though."

Spoon rubs his temples and says, "Mason, go inside and eat."

"Can I have a coffee?" Mason asks.

"Ask her inside."

Hem takes his time getting to his feet. The pressure of the concrete wall has put a knot in his back, and both his legs are numb. He stomps his feet and slaps his knees to bring them back to life.

"Are you letting me out, then?"

For a moment, Spoon seems undecided. Then he shakes his head and steps aside.

Hem picks up his bag and starts to leave, feeling sorry for the dog and hoping she will make it through the birth. He's stepping through the door when Spoon says, "Damn hot. Even way up here. You think we should bring her inside?"

He's crouched down with his hand across the dog's head. She's still too weak to stand. Hem knows he will have to help Spoon carry her, but he takes care to leave his bag outside the kennel. Spoon goes to a shelf near the food bin and retrieves a tattered bath towel, which they use to make a sling. The dog takes to it willingly, lying very still and without complaint. Just outside the kennel, Spoon insists on stopping. They lay the dog on the ground while he re-threads the chain and snaps the heavy lock around it.

Hem says, "You're afraid they'll escape?"

Spoon laughs shortly from the back of his throat and mutters, "They know."

After locking up the door, he stops and stares out at the valley, scratching his face.

"You can have one when she whelps. I'll give you first pick."

Hem says, "That's all right—" but quickly changes his mind. He knows that he can't call on animal control—not when he has been practicing without a license for so long—so he will have to settle for the chance to take at least one dog from Spoon's care.

Spoon grins and slaps him on the back. "You'll look forward to it," he says.

They lift the dog again and carry her up to the house and through another door into the basement. It is shockingly cold. Spoon's house thrums with the sullen rhythm of his air conditioning.

"We'll put her by the fridge," Spoon says. By this, he means the steel chest freezer in the corner. There's nothing else in the room except a torn couch and a huge projection television, which spews yards of colored wires out across the floor.

The dog seems happier inside. She swings her head behind her to sniff underneath the freezer.

"Don't go getting ideas," Spoon says.

He slowly blinks, then puts a hand on Hem's shoulder. "I guess you want to get home to your party."

Hem nods. His head is buzzing, and his skin feels covered in grease. Without another word, Spoon wanders off through a second doorway, leaving Hem to find his own way out. Soon, he hears the thumping of Spoon's heavy boots as he climbs up the stairs.

"I'll return the dog," Spoon calls back. "After you leave."

"Well," Hem says, "Trevor will be happy."

He thinks for a moment. "I'm not tough, you know. But you still needed me."

Spoon laughs and coughs again. "Don't coddle him. It won't go well."

Before he leaves, Hem gives the dog a pill, then kneels beside her for a moment with his eyes closed. In his mind, he follows Spoon upstairs, down a long hallway through the kitchen (where he passes Mason sitting quietly beside his coffee), and then into the den, where he paces back and forth along a well-worn pathway in the rug. He paces like an animal —deliberately but without end.

CHAPTER 49

VALLEY

It is nearly noon when Hem arrives home. From the top of the drive, he can see the yard is littered with toys and strips of purple streamer. There are children standing in a cluster at the edge of the creek, staring down into the water.

Trevor comes to meet him, swinging eagerly across the lawn.

"Dad! You came back!"

"I wouldn't miss your party," Hem says.

After the cool breezes on the road, the stagnant air is stifling. He looks past Trevor to the creek, where Kate is crouching, one arm curled around Sonny's neck.

"Is that Sonny?"

Trevor looks away. "He came last night, but Mom says that we have to tell Mr. Sullivan."

A collective shriek comes from the crowd of kids still bent over the creek. Lorraine stands a few paces behind them, gesturing excitedly towards Hem.

"Dad, we can't send him back."

Hem sets his bag down on the hood and squints into the sun.

"What are they doing over there?"

"Somebody found a snake."

Lorraine has lost her patience and is running towards them. Hem can feel exhaustion's heavy hands press down on him, and he wants to go inside to lie down and forget about Spoon's sick hounds. But he's happy when Lorraine takes his head in her hands and looks at him with apprehension.

"I'm all right," he says.

"Some man called here at two a.m. and said you had to spend the night. I tried to call back, but no one picked up. Then this morning, all these kids just started coming..."

"I'm all right," he says. "Just tired."

He decides that he will never tell her. He will say that it was his decision and will bear the consequences of her anger. This is because he's embarrassed and doesn't think he can bear his family's pity.

She pulls away. "I'm sorry," she says, wiping her eyes. "Here, you came at the perfect time. We need you."

At the creek, the children are excessively excited. Kate lets go of Sonny, who comes up to sniff Hem's hand, snorts once, and trots away.

"They found a snake," Kate says. She looks as tired as he feels, a little haggard, as though she has gone without sleep. She adds hesitantly, "It looks like a northern."

Going to the bank, he pushes two young boys aside and leans out over the stream. The sun is hot and high, and in its light, the water's ripples seem suspended, like translucent sculptures making just the sounds of movement. He can see the snake a short distance away, lying on a rock, with its head pointed downstream. It is all black, slicked with water, and as long as Hem is tall. It seems stunned, paying no attention to the anxious faces hovering above it.

Seeing this awakens something in him. It's not an impulse but a feeling more akin to self-coercion. He's apprehensive even as his foot hangs boldly out above the stream. The snake begins to move, but Hem is faster, bringing his heel down behind its head and pinning it to the creek bed. His boot fills with water as the snake's tail thrashes in the shallows. The children scream and scatter back onto the lawn.

He reaches down into the water and searches for the snake's head. Its tail has sunk beneath the surface, where it lazily whips back and forth.

Making sure he has it just behind the jaw, Hem lifts his foot and pulls it up into the air. Its mouth is open, its soft jaw pushed askew. It hangs limp in his hands as though it recognizes the futility of struggle.

He holds it firmly, just behind its head, and twists until he feels the snap of bone and cartilage, and then he's satisfied.

He drops it, then, and watches it float belly-up downstream.

The children are all quiet. There is no sound but the steady singing of the creek.

The snake floats past the stand of sweet birch that obscures the bend and, catching on another rock, immediately rights itself and swims away.

Hem is happy he's the only one who sees.

"Hem, you have to call the police. What if there'd been no water? What if he hadn't let you out?"

Lorraine is sitting up against the headboard, watching as Hem shoves his face deeper into his pillow.

"George says he's got half of them in his pocket. It wouldn't do any good."

Lorraine knows he's exhausted. She is, too. The difference is she's having trouble calming down. When Hem is tired, and especially when he doesn't feel like talking, he has a way of hiding from her—shutting down and pulling into himself like a turtle. He will answer her, but she knows he is far away, trying hard to force himself to sleep.

"I don't know if you remember," she says, "but the world is a bigger place than Shokten. Some small-town criminal—he can't outweigh the cops. And if he tries, or if he's trying—you can't let him."

Hem grunts. "Let's talk about it in the morning."

"If you don't call, I will."

"Jesus," Hem says, "let it go."

There's a creaking sound from down the hall as Trevor shifts in bed. They've left the windows open, and the night breeze flicks the curtain, making it waft into the room just like a ghost.

Lorraine feels suddenly like, for a long time, she's been waiting. Waiting for a sign—a signal—something to convince her things will change. Still—

"Hem?"

He's breathing more deeply now, and she can hear the faint beginnings of a snore.

Still—she must ask herself why she—so many years ago—so many times—did not leave, why she didn't take the kids back home to Providence. The kids who have both grown so differently out here. Trevor with his broken leg, and Kate with Connor Biel. She has to think that if they grew up in a proper setting, they would be much different. Kate, she knows, would have at least applied to college.

Now, as Hem begins to sleep in earnest, Lorraine lies very much awake, wondering what brought her here. What made her stay? She wonders, years from now—or maybe not so long—if she'll be able to explain. Of course, she wants to tell her children that there is a thing called love—a thing with an existence all its own, outside of human intellect or reason. But she knows that this is only knowledge that she once had. Knowledge that is faded now, eroded by the stream of her experience.

She also knows that there is a possibility of telling them that love isn't what they think it is. That love is often dull and very often does not signal permanence the way that one might like it to.

CHAPTER 50

MOUNTAIN

Lying on his back in bed, Mason holds himself stone still despite the heat. He listens for the mountain's call, afraid that it has been so long since he last heard it that he has forgotten its sound. Maybe all of his attempts to reach out through the darkness, though the cloying summer air and smell of agitated dogs are no more useful than his past attempts to see the outside world. Maybe his perceptions and experiences are not something he can conjure as he chooses to, no matter how he tries. Wide awake but disgusted with his mind's incessant focus on itself, he shuts his eyes and tries to give himself away to the coarse touch of his sheets and to the sprays of blue-and-black lights that fade in and out beneath his eyelids. They are feather-light; they fall apart and coalesce. The air he breathes is hot, but it is solid—firm enough, he thinks, to hold almost anything aloft. He's aware of his desire to get out of bed, though by the time he is within sight of the kennel, the memory has been overlaid with so many similar moments that it has become difficult to recognize.

The trap is still behind the kennel, in the shadow cast by moonlight on the eaves. As he approaches, he hears something move inside—a rustle from the feathers of a pigeon lying at the bottom of the cage. It has been here for three days, and it does not alarm at Mason's presence. He kneels down to look into its small black eyes, but they are closed against him. He tries hard to recall how he meant to get the bird out of the cage once he had caught it, but he can't. It doesn't matter anyway. He won't need it anymore. Carefully, he reaches out and flips the latch that drops the cage door. The bird's eyes open, and it rises halfway to its feet, only to settle down again. Cursing, Mason rattles the cage. The pigeon only lifts its wings enough to steady itself against the rocking. He grabs the back of the cage and lifts it upside down, shaking it until the bird flops out onto the ground.

"Get going," Mason says. His teeth are clenched. He pushes the bird forward with his toe. It makes a soft, frightened trill and topples over on its side.

Furious, he kicks out. The bird's claws scratch against his ankle. He leans in and stomps upon it, tentatively at first, then harder, moving from its body to its head, until he hears its bones snap underneath his heel. Panting now, he backs away and cleans his foot off in the dirt. Feathers rise and fall around him in the breeze. He sees a pattern in them, a reproachful message in a language he cannot quite understand. In bursts of rage, he kicks both bird and trap over the mountain's edge, only calming as he watches them both tumble down into the darkness. He goes slowly home, with each step growing more aware of a dissatisfaction that is fast becoming the most recognizable of his emotions.

Mason doesn't want the mountain, and he doesn't want the world. Neither one is as he had expected it to be. Neither is as he imagines it.

CHAPTER 51

KATE

When they were children, she and Trevor used to play a game.

In the basement of her father's practice, there was an industrial furnace. She doesn't know how it got there —whether it came with the building or if her father had it installed—but it's one of those strange sights from childhood that stopped her short, crawled in through her eyes, and made a home in her forever.

The furnace ran all day and late into the night when Hem would finally lock things up and come home. One of them (she or Trevor) would stand beside the furnace, facing towards the shimmer of the steel door. The other would go up the steps onto the first floor and, from there, shut off the lights.

Kate doesn't know what it was like for Trevor, but for her, the trek back up the stairs was serious—a journey and a meditation. In the dark, her scattered thoughts seemed more important, more her own. If she tried hard enough, she could forget who or what she was and let herself go, following every impulse she had been accustomed to checking.

When Trevor turned the lights off, a red light burst

around the edges of the door. One night, while she was staring into this, the basement lights switched on, and Hem came down to find her standing there, looking very guilty. In his hands, he held a small, taut plastic bag.

He said, "What are you doing? You should go back upstairs."

She was silent until finally, Hem shrugged and turned a knob. The hissing from inside the furnace slowly quieted. When Hem unlocked the door, the heat that flew at her was just as terrible and satisfying as she had imagined.

Grimacing, her father flung the bag inside and shut the door. He turned the knob the other way, and the furnace sprang back into life.

Now, of course, she knows the game was cruel. Trevor wasn't old enough to understand and only played because he knew if he refused, she would abandon him.

She remembers wanting to look in the bag before Hem threw it in—remembers thinking that there could be anything inside of it—her father did not care.

There is no selflessness in caring for a loved one. If it were not in our best interest, we would never take the job. That is how things work beneath the surface, underneath ourselves. Nothing equals selfishness in its capacity to do all kinds of good.

CHAPTER 52

DOCTOR

Beneath the harsh fluorescent lights, Trevor's leg seems coated with a grisly yellow sheen. Cole handles it with a detached intensity, raising it and bending it, stroking and massaging, all the time disturbing little scaly bits of luminescent skin, which flutter down onto the table. He points out a lump on Trevor's shin, which he doesn't think will resolve.

"It may look awful now," he says, "but it's cosmetic. It won't slow him down at all."

"The scars of battle," Hem says.

"Yes."

Cole bends and lays a hand on Trevor's chest.

"Be careful with it for a while. Definitely stay away from bulls."

They both help Trevor off the table and onto his feet. He puts his full weight on the leg without a grimace.

"Does it feel good?" Hem asks.

Trevor nods. "Much better."

"So," says Cole, "Spoon says you fixed that precious dog of his."

Hem starts.

"I guess I did. You're friends?"

Cole shrugs.

"When you're the only doctor, you eventually get to know everyone in town. Anyway, he's got high hopes for that dog. Or I should say, for the puppies. Are they really worth what he thinks? It's a bit hard to believe."

Hem shakes his head, and Cole begins to smile.

"You don't know," Hem says. "He'll kill them when he finds out what they are."

As though he has been waiting for this, Cole's grin cracks and bursts into a laugh.

"How far the mighty fall," he says, while Hem can only stare, and Trevor glances back and forth between the two of them, wondering what he has missed.

At the front desk, Hem signs papers. Cole leans close and asks him if the daydreams have stopped.

Hem pauses, then says, "What you gave me—"

"It's not working."

"No, not mostly."

"I can give you something else. Something stronger. Something different, at the very least. Or you might just try relaxing. Fish. Take long walks."

"Maybe."

As he slides the papers back across the desk to the receptionist, Hem already begins imagining his walk. In the early morning, first light—stepping off the porch into the dying song of crickets and the sound of branches moving in the trees —down the path beside the barn and down the long drive— dirt beneath him, hardly dressed—out onto the road, from Shokten to the sea.

Later, on the main road, Trevor swings his leg up on the dash and prods the bony lump on his shin. Hem's window faces towards the river—Trevor's, at the tall and dusky cliffs of shale. They follow this path for another mile through what seems a thicket of sunbeams, parting before them like grass.

At the first curve in the road and river, they can see the Eubanks' farm. The pasture is a little overgrown, but it's spotted with a number of handsome Shorthorn cows.

Trevor straightens when Hem turns the station wagon off the main road.

"Are we going to see Eustace?"

Hem says, "I should check in now that you're all better. George will never call again if I don't."

Trevor scratches the welt behind his knee, where the dead skin is thickest.

"Why'd you kill the snake?" he says.

Hem rolls down the window, searching for the smell of smoke and leaves that signal fall. He wants that comfort.

"It was dangerous. You know that."

"We would all have stayed away from it."

"And Sonny?"

"Him too."

Hem parks in the grass beside the house. When he shuts the engine off, it makes a sound like water boiling. He shuts his eyes and rubs them lightly.

"Sometimes it feels good to kill," he says. "Sometimes, it makes you feel like you deserve to live."

In dreams, some men live lives without shame, without fear, and without their unremitting, selfish lust for beauty. Unencumbered by the need to ask why. In dreams.

There is a knock from outside, and they turn to see Mica smirking at them through the rear window. She has traded in her sundress for a pair of tight jeans and a T-shirt.

"George is out," she says, arms crossed, her body resting easily against the jamb.

"We came to check on Eustace."

"Well, I'm leaving soon, but you can go and see him if you want." She looks at Trevor. "How's the leg?"

Trevor stretches it towards her. It has turned from green to gray but still looks luminescent and covered with scales.

"You can touch it if you want," he says.

Hem puts a hand on the back of Trevor's neck. "She doesn't want to touch it. Let's go see the bull, and then we'll leave her alone."

Mica squats and looks intently into Trevor's eyes.

"You're not scared?"

Hem is touched by her sincerity.

"I shouldn't have run behind him," Trevor says.

"It was an accident, you know."

Mica stands, retracting her attention just as quickly as she gave it. "Leave the barn door open, will you? Eustace likes the breeze."

Hem watches as she walks off and shakes an image from his head. He thinks again of how much she reminds him of Kate. They both seem so completely unaware of what they do not know.

Summer's heat has baked the field into a pitted sheet of clay. Hem stumbles at the bottom of a hardened hoof print and turns to find that Trevor is a dozen yards behind him. While he waits, he takes a careful interest in his son's disjointed gait. It seems to take his weight just fine, but Trevor is afraid of hurting it and keeps on dragging it beside him, tapping only lightly, like a blind man's stick. Hem hopes Cole has done a good job. He can't imagine how Lorraine will take it if she finds out there is any lasting damage.

They go on at Trevor's pace, in silence, until they reach the barn door. Eustace wakes up at the sound of hinges, shaking off the black flies that have gathered on him, taking full advantage of his nap.

Hem looks at Trevor, who is watching through the crack. "You don't have to come in," he says.

"I want to," says Trevor, but doesn't move. The cows are grunting in the field, and Eustace seems to sigh along with them.

"For what it's worth, he doesn't care. He doesn't even remember."

Trevor nods. He sets his jaw and steps into the barn, his eyes fixed deliberately on the bull.

Hem steps back, giving them the private space that he believes they need. As Trevor reaches out and splays his hand between the bull's broad nostrils, Hem can't help but think that Kate wouldn't have shown this same respect. To her, he thinks, the bull is just an animal—completely irresponsible and listless. When he turned the car into the Eubanks' drive, she would have balked. She has no sympathy for nature, no appreciation for differences of degree.

Eustace snorts and stomps his feet, and Trevor smiles.

"I'm assuming that was sorry," he says.

Hem believes in difference, and the differences he sees between his children boil down to this: Kate came into the world limp and silent—so that someone had to smack her to make sure she was alive—while Trevor came out screaming like a barn cat. Watching his small hand pressed up against the bull, Hem feels the satisfaction of communion. He becomes more certain that the world is a navigable place. He believes there is a unity confounding all appearance.

It's not until Kate meets her doctor that she feels the first small pangs of worry. It occurs to her, as Cole walks past her, sitting on the table in the flimsy gown the nurse provided, and begins to wash his hands, that making life is complicated. Not the simple act she had imagined it to be, but something with a clear potential for catastrophe. Something that required doctors and their offices, the constant testing and debate that seems more suited to an illness than the natural products of desire.

Doctor Cole is quiet, as though there's something on his mind. He has been Kate's doctor since they moved to Shokten, though she hasn't seen him regularly in years. She's surprised to find the man she knew—an apple-cheeked and silly young man, brimming with curiosity about the lives of all his patients—transformed into a brooding, melancholy adult.

"I haven't seen you in a while," he says.

"I guess there's not much to go wrong with kids."

He laughs. "No. It tends to be the accidental things that get them. Keeps you on your toes."

After washing his hands, he dries them carefully with a paper towel. Above his head hang two elaborate degrees in white frames.

"You must have been in school a long time," she says.

He nods slowly. "Two degrees. It wasn't hard. I had fun."

"Fun! Well, it must be boring out here, then."

"In some ways."

He tells her to lie down and opens up her gown without asking.

"I wouldn't want to go back to Providence if that's what you mean. Too smothering."

"You don't miss the excitement?"

He grins. "Oh, that's just grass-is-greener thinking. There's more excitement here than Providence if you know where to look."

Kate sighs. "I haven't found it yet."

"Well," he says. "It's early still, but let's see if we can't find a heartbeat, shall we?"

Kate nods. Until now, she has been thinking of the baby as inanimate—a little gang of cells clinging to her in the darkness.

"I didn't think it had one yet."

"It does," Cole smirks. "Nine months isn't long, so Mother Nature has to rush."

She recognizes the small monitor, like the toy amplifiers she and Trevor used to sing into as kids.

"A little cold," Cole says, squeezing clear gel on her stomach, just below her navel. She sucks in a breath, hoping it will help the microphone pick up whatever evidence her child can provide that it is real.

Cole moves the knob, and soon the room fills with a sound like water rushing through her ears.

"Is that him?" Kate asks.

"Him? You sound so certain."

Kate's cheeks flush. "I'm sorry. I guess I've just been hoping."

"I suppose your father's happy?"

Kate sighs. "I don't think he's ever all that happy."

The doctor leans in closer to the little speaker and listens.

"Well, it isn't him," he says. "That's just your blood. But —" he moves the knob again, and she can hear a faint beat— someone tapping on an empty shell.

"How does that feel?" Cole asks.

She's a little stricken and takes her time. It feels like the world has suddenly gained another light. Like she has topped a ridge, she has been climbing for a long time and is gazing out at some new land, where things take on a brightness they never had before.

"It's wonderful."

He snaps off the machine, and she's suddenly brought back to the ground.

"So."

She lies still, with her body still exposed. He hasn't told her yet if they are finished.

"I suppose we need to talk about some things you should

start and—I'm just guessing here—some things that you should stop."

"I know I shouldn't drink," she says, thinking of the pint she put away the night before. It isn't that she doesn't care. She just gets lonely on the days when Connor's gone—days that have begun to bleed together like the pattern on a quilt. She supposes she has spent too much time around her father, learning that all living bodies—even small ones—are much more resilient than most people give them credit for.

"Yes, and" he stares directly at her for the first time. "Other things as well."

She stares back, put off by the level-headed seriousness in his eyes. He holds this just a moment longer, hovering above her like a puppet, then breaks his stare and goes quickly to the sink.

"I'm not insinuating anything," he says softly. "There are just—a lot of things in this town that can ruin your health."

"I understand," she says, sitting up and tying her gown. But she doesn't really. For the first time, she wonders if her father was right. If the whole town knows about how Connor spends his weekends.

"Listen," Cole says, drying off his hands. "Everything looks fine. Just keep taking your vitamins, eating well, and so on. And if you find yourself in need of anything—I mean, anything that I can give you, let me know."

Kate nods. "Thank you."

"Congratulations," he says, then taps her quickly on the shoulder and leaves the room.

CHAPTER 53

PLAYGROUND

They are huddled up inside the wooden ship out on the playground, though they are supposed to be in class. Lily has been urging him to skip, and he has reached the point at which he can't say no without making her angry. It is cool inside the ship, back in the shadows of its bow, in the smell of damp pine mulch and rust.

Lily says, "Trevor says your dad locked you in a kennel with his dogs."

He looks hard into her eyes and tries to see what answer she is hoping for. Her face is half in light and half in shade; her eyes dart back and forth between the two uncertainly.

"He locks a lot of people in the kennel. Not for very long. They're all fine when they get out."

She shifts closer to him in the pine chips and the dust.

"So, he lets them out."

"Yes," says Mason. "Always."

"But still, he puts them in there. What for? Don't they pay him?"

He has trouble concentrating on her question when she

tilts her head so that the thin light from the gangway falls across her neck, which is stretched and bare.

"I don't know," he says.

"You don't know!"

"He doesn't tell me anything."

She squints her eyes up into his. "Why?"

"Because I'm just a kid."

"You are not!"

Lily pitches forward on her hands and knees and stares very intently at him. "You can't be once you've seen the things you have." Blinking furiously, she waves a hand, fluttering it through the small space between them. "Your dad's drugs, his dogs, his..." she searches for something else. "You know, the way he treats your mom."

It is now he knows she isn't at all interested in him, as he first thought, or in his story, as he began to think later on, but only in the confirmation of a story she has ready-made for him —a story scraped together out of years of local rumors and hearsay. This knowledge comes to him suddenly and unavoidably: a juggernaut, and suddenly the ship's hold seems much larger, filled with light, and Lily smaller, a mere girl now, not crouched but cowering inside it.

CHAPTER 54

VALLEY

Lorraine has spent the day out walking by the creek. This morning, Hem took Trevor fishing. They left long before she woke up. In the past, she would have been quite happy, knowing they were spending time together. In the past, she would have had Kate. They would walk together, talking and sharing things the way she thinks Hem and Trevor must be doing now. Just sitting somewhere, talking, and letting time go by.

She's letting time go by, too. Not the way she has done—accidentally—but purposely, the way she used to do, she thinks, when she and Hem were first together. And no, it's more than that. The way she used to let time slip away when she was young, before she met Hem and before her life became the mesh of people and responsibilities that it has now become.

There was a time, she thinks, when she could walk along the creek, and there would be the creek, and her, and nothing else.

That time is long past. Now, there is the creek, but there is Hem, and there are Trevor and Kate. They follow her despite her wishes. They whisper in her ears and ruin things. They make her walk a kind of pilgrimage—a search for answers rather than, as she remembers, in the glory days, a search for questions.

Along the creek, the ferns are falling, dropping leaves into the current. She watches as they spin away downstream, not caring where they go. She's thinking of a day when she was little, playing in the creek behind her grandparents' house. She had liked collecting minnows in a bucket, then swirling the water to watch them swim against the current.

Far downriver, she sees Hem and Trevor, two hunched shadows on the bank. It's afternoon, and they'll be tired soon, so she begins the long walk back to wait for them at home. She has decided to call the police.

CHAPTER 55

SHOKTEN

The smell of mildew is so thick under the porch that Trevor has to breathe through his sleeve. His crutches are wedged awkwardly beside him, one caught in a web of chicken wire, the other balanced across his lap. Mason sits hunched against the concrete wall, knees drawn up, arms tight around them. The space is barely tall enough to sit in, and only wide enough for the two of them to fit if they lean slightly sideways. Trevor doesn't know whose porch it is–he only ran for the closest hiding spot available.

"They're gone," Mason says, but doesn't sound convinced.

Trevor stares at the thin slit of daylight between the floorboards above them, waiting for a shadow to move across it. Nothing. Just bird sounds. Wind in the fence.

"What'd you see?" he asks.

Mason shrugs, then wipes his hands on his jeans. "Spoon's truck. And two guys I don't know."

Trevor tries to slow his breathing. His side still hurts from the fall. His bad leg twitches, already sore from hobbling too fast over the ridge when Mason shouted for him to run.

He says, "Why would they come here?"

Mason doesn't answer. His hair is stuck to his forehead. His eyes keep flicking towards the opening.

After a minute, Trevor says, "Is it about your dad?"

"Maybe."

"Or you?"

Mason shrugs again.

Silence stretches. It isn't still—it vibrates with things neither of them will say. Trevor presses the crutch tighter against his chest and feels the soft edge of panic rising behind his ribs.

"Are they mad about something?"

"Probably."

"What'd you do?"

"I feed the dogs now. That's what I do."

Trevor frowns. "That's not an answer."

Mason shifts. The dry rustle of leaves under him sounds too loud. "They don't need reasons. You ever met someone like that?"

Trevor doesn't answer. His stomach twists.

He thinks about Sonny. About Kate leaving. About his dad staring at the fireplace like something might crawl out of it if he waits long enough.

He says, "What's it like... at your house?"

Mason closes his eyes. "It's like if you live in a mine long enough, you start forgetting there's an outside."

Trevor tries to picture it. He can't. He only knows the edge of it—the smell of it clinging to Mason's jacket, the way his voice flattens when he talks about home.

"Does your mom ever talk to you?"

"She sings sometimes. When she's high."

"Do you ever think about leaving?"

Mason opens one eye. "No. That's a thing your sister does."

Trevor smiles, then doesn't. "She's not coming back."

"I know."

The floorboards groan above them. Both boys freeze. A squirrel darts across the beams and disappears.

Trevor lets out a breath. "I thought—"

"I know."

They wait another minute. Then Mason shifts towards the crawl space opening and listens.

"Coast is clear."

Trevor hesitates. "You sure?"

"No."

They crawl out anyway. The grass is wet. The light looks too sharp, like everything's been on pause and just now started again. Trevor grips the edge of the porch and pulls himself up slowly. His leg trembles.

Mason helps him balance. Their shadows stretch long behind them.

CHAPTER 56

VALLEY

The police take over an hour to arrive. When they do, Hem is upstairs helping Trevor with his homework.

There is only one officer, a young woman with her hair pulled tight against her scalp.

"Are you the one who called?"

Lorraine nods. She is suddenly self-conscious.

"I just have to get my husband. Do you want to come in?"

She leaves the officer standing by the kitchen door and goes to find Hem. He's in the upstairs hallway on his way back from the bathroom.

"Who's here?" he asks.

"Listen Hem...I called the police."

His attitude shifts immediately. She can see it in the way his tensing muscles raise him up an inch.

"You called the cops? I told you not to."

"Hem, I don't know what to say. He locked you in a kennel."

"That's right, so what do you think he'll do if I tell them?"

"Well," she says," "I guess we'll find out. They're not going to leave now."

She has to admit that as he pushes past her, he looks like a man on his way to the gallows. She follows, fighting a sudden feeling that he might do something unusual. Something so far outside of what she believes she can predict that he, for her, will cease to be Hem and set her free.

Downstairs, the officer is on her radio.

"I hear you," she says. "I'm on a call."

The radio clicks off, and she replaces it on her hip.

"Hello," Hem says. Not angrily, but as if he has been defeated in some way.

"So, can you tell me what happened?" She touches a notebook in her breast pocket but does not remove it.

"It was really an accident," Hem says. "Mr. Sullivan was drunk. He locked the kennel so the dogs wouldn't escape, then forgot about it until the next morning."

The officer laughs. "I'm not surprised to hear he was drunk."

Hem laughs along with her. Uneasily, but looking slightly hopeful.

"That sounds uncomfortable," she says, "but more like a mistake than a crime."

Lorraine holds her tongue. She should have known that Hem would have a story ready. She supposes that she didn't expect him to care this much. During this exchange, she has opened her mouth more than once but isn't sure she wants to have this argument aired all over town.

The officer turns to her.

"The story you told dispatch went a little differently."

"Well," Lorraine says. She's privately seething. "Even if it was an accident, I hope you'll at least give him a warning."

The officer nods and looks at Hem. "You don't want to press charges, then."

"That won't be necessary," Hem says.

She has never felt anger like this. Or perhaps the new

sensation comes from holding it in check, allowing it to rise and rise until her hands are trembling.

Hem escorts the woman out and returns, obviously relieved. "Look," he begins, "she said they'll say something—a warning, like you said."

She stares at him and sees a ghost.

"Hem, next time, he could kill someone."

"I understand, I do. But you don't think about the consequences."

"I know all about what may or may not happen. I'm just man enough to face it."

CHAPTER 57

FAY

Fay is often frightened by the things that children think are possible. An hour ago, she was coming down, and already upset, Mason asked if they could move.

"Move?" she said. "Where?"

"I don't know. The city?"

Recently, she has been having trouble distinguishing between her imagination and reality. The world as she sees it seems to be a blend of things and of her noticing, of ragged, horrifyingly imperfect sense.

"If we leave," she says, "we might not find our way back."

Mason, with his face a boiler, his face a teardrop, and an urn, appears to understand. He looks down at his shoes, squats, rises, says, "Okay," and leaves her standing by the window, watching sea-haze settle in the valley, wondering how it would feel to fall, to give in, give up, lay it all down.

She believes that there is nothing she can do. Her son will turn out like his father.

"Mason!"

She has set her hands against the window pane and thinks that she can feel it tremble as he paces in his room.

"Mason!"

It gives her a headache. She sucks in breath, but carefully, the way a diver gets prepared to live beneath the sea. And then she lets it out—a crashing "MASON!"—that is like the bellow of a bull.

Upstairs, there is a pause, and then the sound of feet. Quick and hollow on the stairs, coming down to meet her.

Chapter 58

Kate

Kate sits by the window, waiting to see Connor's headlights flashing through the trees. She knows that when they do, they will illuminate the spoils of last weekend's party—cigarette butts, bottles, greasy paper plates—still scattered on the lawn. She has no idea where he is and treats her ignorance with tea and alcohol like a sickness. She has told herself that when he comes home, she will ask him. She will tell him that she needs to know—the things he does, the way he gets his money. Too much money for a miner. Just too much to keep him honest.

For now, the night is dark and empty, save for fireflies and the occasional bright wave of moonlight.

Now she's thinking of the first time she and Connor had sex, back when it was still an act that both of them believed in. When they finished, Connor lay spread out and naked on the bed beneath the slowly spinning ceiling fan. His eyelids shuddered, and there was coal dust in his lashes. At the time, she thought it was romantic—him laid out that way because of her—exhausted in a way that even long days underground, breathing bad air, breathing diesel, cleaning belts, and hacking at the face, could ever seem to match. She believed that it was hers—that helplessness, that ease.

Blue light from the street lamps made blue ripples in the sheets. She touched him, and he batted her away. She ran a finger carefully across his lashes, where the dust seemed stuck for good.

"Now quit," he said.

"Why don't you ever clean them?"

"I'm too tired from trying."

She's fascinated by his body. She would like to run her knuckles down his side, over each one of his ribs from top to bottom, to find exactly where they stop. But he shoves her off again, rises, and starts to search around the bed, looking for wherever he has dropped his clothes. She considers how much past there is to love and how hard it has been to remember the present.

He will come home soon, already drunk, and he will think she is upset. He will rub her back and whisper songs and hand her some poor rock or chestnut he has found, trying in his way to make her better. But he won't know that the alcohol has done its work. She isn't angry. She will ask no questions. For the moment, she is happy, thinking of the tree she used to wait beside—a full pine, glossy with night—and of the way that he was once splayed out across her bed, exhausted.

CHAPTER 59

MARCH

March discovers that the eyehole on his broken fishing pole fits perfectly around the heads of all the nails protruding from his porch. He tries to lift them, but the ring is weak and bends under the pressure. He sticks his tongue between his teeth and grimaces, then throws the pole into the yard, where it's caught, suspended in the long grass. Slumping on the steps, his eyes begin to close.

There are times—not now—but times when he believes in things outside himself. In God, though fleetingly; in man, though fitfully; and often, when he is awake and horribly alert, in something he perhaps believes in but is not prepared to know. A secret: that the world is both singular and multiple. That there is not I, there is not It, there is not We, there is not They—there is All—there is a mash—there is a unity confounding all appearance.

He can still see Lucky, with her head stuck underneath the porch, her tail behind her like a flag.

"You," he says. The sound of it appears to shiver through his bones instead of through his throat.

"You think too much about death."

He remembers.

Sitting on their freshly mown lawn, drinking mai-tais from a plastic thermos. Cathleen saying, "What else is a husband for?" The thermos is empty, and she wants another drink.

The dog's eyes roll up at the sound of March's voice. He has entered the penultimate, uncertain part of his day, which lies between the bottle's halfway point and its damp bottom.

It is August, and the river is a slick brown ribbon flossing perfectly within its banks. March picks up the thermos and goes back across the lawn and up the porch steps into the house. He gets the orange juice and syrup out of the refrigerator and begins to mix in rum. He hears the crash but doesn't pause to wonder. His hands stay steady. He's proud that he doesn't spill even one drop. Back onto the porch then, thermos shaking, for the moment when he sees the oak tree lying sideways where his wife had been.

"Listen," March says.

He remembers.

"Just because we know about it doesn't mean we can't ignore it."

Years ago, alone (Cathleen went off to visit relatives), just listening to rain and drinking in an effort to ignore the gray scum rising through the cracked linoleum. The kitchen is full of dishes. Half a chicken wrapped in paper and a pistol on the table. Smelling moss and rot.

Then the yapping. Faint at first. Just a twitch behind the rain. But steady. Rising. Unmistakable.

He couldn't help it—had to hear. Had to know.

"I might have," March says. Meaning, as he usually does, he might have saved more than one. If he'd been faster. If he'd had the sense to stay sober. If he'd remembered to take off his boots.

He forgot about his boots, which quickly turned to lead.

And he forgot the river wasn't where it should be. He thought they'd all get caught up in the eel trap at the bend. By the time he got there, one squirming pup tucked in against his chest, there was no trap, no bend. Just floodplain. Water pressing through the trees, wide and brown and everywhere.

"And all from anger. All from spite."

She's not wrong to be angry. But this? The years she spent digging circles around that tree, like it held some secret pocket of truth or punishment. He never told her that he kept the boots. That they still smell like that night. He knows he deserves some punishment, but he's only one man—he can't dig that deep.

For the hundredth time, March searches in her eyes and in his heart and finds forgiveness.

He believes dumb animals can't help but think dumb thoughts.

Chapter 60

Playground

Trevor is a good boy and obedient. He never leaves his class for any reason other than to use the bathroom. Though he sometimes lingers, listening to echoes he can create inside the empty hallways or admiring the brown mold growing on the tiles just outside the gym, he always makes sure to return within the limits of his teachers' expectations.

Which is why, today, he feels that he has taken an unreasonable risk. He hobbles through the hallways, horribly aware of every sound his crutches make against the vinyl flooring.

He adjusts his shirt so that the newest sweat stains underneath his arms are towards the back. Then he turns his head around, casting up and down the hallway for a feeling he believes he has when friends are near. It is something like hope, but while hope is just rocking in his head and chest, this feeling is a pointed urge, more like ambition. Trevor feels it strongly when he looks behind him towards the doors that lead out to the playground.

He has noticed Mason's frequent absences and can't understand why teachers do not seem to mind. Trevor likes to think of Mason as a person who is very lost and desperately in need.

The empty playground frightens him. He feels the hopeful feeling pointing into it, and then he hears the sound of Lily's laughter from the wooden ship beside the swings.

It isn't easy swinging crutches through a field of rubber, but at least it stifles any hint of his approach.

There is a place behind the stern where he can lean and see into the hull. Mason sits erect while Lily leans dramatically against his arm. They talk in whispers, but the hollow chamber amplifies their conversation.

"It's not his fault," Mason says. "It's hers."

"What do you mean?"

"She never does what she's supposed to."

"Oh."

"She sleeps all day and never makes us food. Or sometimes she's awake and won't leave anyone alone."

"It must be hard."

Mason looks out through the doorway at the span of rubber fill. If Trevor tries, he knows that he can make their eyes meet. It would be like looking in a mirror that shows you who you cannot ever be.

Now Mason reaches out for Lily's hand. She gives it to him, and he places it securely between his legs.

CHAPTER 61

KATE

The burn pile at the edge of the yard still smokes from the storm. A few sticks hiss where the rain didn't reach. Kate toes in a piece of charred plywood, then sits on the overturned bucket Connor has rolled over from the shed.

He stands a little ways off, tapping a rusted shovel against the ground, not digging, not doing anything. Just shifting weight.

"Something smells," she says.

"Probably us."

She looks up. "Not funny."

"I wasn't trying."

The sky's the color of wet chalk. Trevor's rocket lies half-buried by the barn, nose cone snapped. The field still hasn't dried. Every corner of the valley seems held together by mildew and string.

Kate wraps her arms around her middle. She isn't showing yet, not really, but her body has begun to feel like someone else's. The baby's not moving yet, but she imagines she can feel it anyway—something turning inside her, slow and underwater.

"I don't think he'll ever say anything," she says.

"Who?"

"My dad."

Connor shrugs. "He doesn't have to."

Hem's silence is its own kind of speech. She knows that already. Still, she hates how it seeps into things—furniture, food, and her decisions.

They listen to the occasional drip from the eaves, the sizzle of wet ash.

"I feel like if I stay, something will start to rot," she says. "Like I'll go sour."

"You think it hasn't already?"

It's not cruel, the way he says it. Just level. Like truth measured by weight.

She doesn't answer. Her hands curl into fists inside her jacket sleeves. Lorraine has started saving bread bags again. Trevor's been sleeping with the light on. And Hem spends whole afternoons just staring into his mug like it might suddenly return to him full of the past.

"So what? You want me to run?"

"No," he says. "Not unless you do."

Neither of them speaks for a minute. Then he says, "What if we did?"

She says, "Did what?"

"Left."

Kate shakes her head, half-laughing. "You don't even know where."

"I don't care."

The smoke folds back on itself, wind-shifted. She tastes ash on her tongue. Thinks about her mother's coat hanging in the hall closet. The drawer with her ultrasound. The dog curled in Trevor's bed.

She says, "That's not a plan."

"Didn't say it was."

Connor drops the shovel and walks towards the house without looking back. Halfway there, he turns and says, "You coming?"

Kate doesn't answer. She watches the last ember on the pile pulse, then vanish. Her throat tastes like ash.

She stands, wipes her hands on her jeans, and follows him in.

They don't talk about it again that night. But the idea stays.

CHAPTER 62

LORRAINE

Lorraine dries her hands on the hem of her shirt and leans into the sink. The window over the basin is streaked from the last storm—mud flecks and long tails of pollen blown in sideways. She doesn't bother wiping it. The view is clear enough.

Out by the burn pile, Kate and Connor sit like they've forgotten how to move. Connor is just standing there holding a shovel like he's thinking of digging his way out.

She opens the window a few inches. Smoke drifts in, warm and faintly sour. The smell wraps itself around the steam from the dishwater and the citrus cleaner she uses when she wants to feel like something's being fixed.

She leans on the sill and watches.

Connor shifts his weight. Says something. Kate doesn't laugh this time. They've been quieter lately. Not distant, not cold. Just... *settled*, like people on a boat watching the shore slip away.

Lorraine knows that look. She wore it once, when she was nineteen and full of schemes about music school in the city. Before Hem. Before the third miscarriage. Before Providence turned into a place she referenced the way some people referenced planets.

They're talking now. Kate folds her arms the way she does when she's hiding nerves—presses her elbows in, eyes narrowed like she's trying to feel the future with her skin. Lorraine can't hear the words, but she doesn't need to. She sees the moment the silence opens up wide between them, and something new drops in.

Connor walks away first, shovel forgotten. Doesn't storm off—just moves like someone finished with the thought. Kate stays sitting. Doesn't call after him.

Lorraine closes the window. She doesn't want Kate to know she's been worried.

Behind her, the kettle begins to hum. The smell of smoke lingers and gets in her throat. She doesn't clear it. She thinks about asking Hem if he's noticed anything. Then she imagines his answer—some clumsy shrug and a mutter about tea—and decides against it. Kate's standing now. Heading in. Her boots leave wet half-moons on the porch before she disappears through the back door. Lorraine stays in the kitchen another minute, watching the steam rise from the sink.

She thinks: *They've already left. Their bodies just haven't caught up yet.*

CHAPTER 63

BAR

Of course, it's a lukewarm beer that finally drives Spoon to unconsidered violence.

He's sitting at his table in his bar. March is on his right, Flint Pearson on his left. They are watching an old, alcoholic miner who is slowly falling off his chair.

"That's us, one day," March says.

Flint sips his whiskey. "Doesn't look too bad to me."

"That's because there's nothing better to look forward to."

Lately, Spoon has been having some trouble keeping his emotions in check. Anger, sadness, apprehension, guilt, uncertainty, despair, and overconfidence—they all arrive like banshees, unannounced, and screaming bloody murder.

He has moved the Pharaoh hound back to the kennel, where she seems to be regaining health. Still, he sees no sign that she's getting ready to give birth. It would be easiest for him to think that Cole has duped him or to blame Hem for incompetence, but he knows that neither is the case, and this infuriates him. He's looking for an outlet.

It is midnight, and the bar is relatively quiet. Things won't heat up until the legal places close and men come looking for a fight. Finally, the old man topples to the floor. His eyes fly open, and he lies there for a moment, staring, then tries unsuccessfully to rise. March and Flint look on impassively, their faces coated with a fine film of disgust.

Spoon keeps two waitresses, both small, poor and eager. One of them stops on her way back from the bar, sets her tray of beer down on the floor, and helps the old man to his feet. He totters back up to the bar, holds on, and sticks his lip out at the bottles. A few young miners offer him a drink, and he accepts. They order something strong and awful—rot-gut gin and cherry rum and licorice schnapps. The old man sets his mouth around the glass's rim and throws it back.

The second waitress comes with Spoon's next beer. She sets the glass down, and he wraps his hand around it. Right away, he knows it doesn't feel right. It is warm and greasy. Flat, no head. A film of soap scum all around the edge.

He stands up, pours the beer onto her chest, and does his best to shove the empty glass straight down her throat. The glass is heavy, and her mouth is small, so after many tries, he only manages to snap her teeth off at the gum, making her red lips black and swollen. Blood flies. Men around him scream. He keeps on pounding at her, unaware, until March finally succeeds in tackling him to the floor.

Spoon fights him off and stands up, straddling the girl's body.

"You all see!" he's shouting. "You all see!"

His forehead bulges as he waves his finger wildly about.

"That fucking bitch!"

But he hardly remembers why he's mad. His anger has become a river he is lost in.

"Listen," March says. "Get her to a hospital."

Suddenly, the river bumps him, and his thoughts diffuse around him, then continue on alone. He has lost his ego, and his anger turns to fright.

Spoon's face and hands are smeared with blood. The glass has broken, spreading shards across the floor. He kneels on these but doesn't mind. He's content with his transcendent feeling of release, in which every twitching cell relaxes, almost as if it were sleeping.

A few men lift the girl up and carry her outside. The rest go back to drinking, slowly at first, then with an excited urgency, which leads them, hours later, to a state of carelessness that they did not mean to attain.

Spoon sits still in the corner with his eyes closed, caught in the elastic space between his roaming mind and the dead weight of his tired body. He begins to dream about a girl he once knew named Sylvie Paw. She was the daughter of Leroy, the man who built the shack that now serves as Spoon's bar. Long ago, when the peninsula's first politicians drew the lines that separate the three municipalities, they accidentally left a spit of land beside the river's mouth untouched. Assured that no authorities were willing to contest his claim, Leroy set up shop. He sold white liquor and a powerful, addicting sedative that he had shipped from Canada, where he had family in the trade. Sylvie was the daughter of a prostitute who died soon after birth. As Sylvie grew, Leroy grew increasingly unstable, and the day she turned fifteen, he ran three miles to the sea and drowned himself.

Spoon was just a child then, but he can still remember going with his father to the bar to offer Sylvie cash. And he remembers Sylvie bending down to bring his face to hers and say, "Your father doesn't know I'm crazy." Her breath was cool and smelled like cider whiskey. After, she began to wear a pistol on her hip—a six-inch Python with a rubber grip. Once, after dusk, Spoon followed her down to the beach. He watched her stand atop a dune and fire eighteen rounds into the sea. Now, this is how he best remembers her—her face illuminated briefly by the muzzle flash, her long legs set against the wind, calmly watching every bullet swallowed up without a sound.

Spoon told his father, who looked down at him and said, "That Leroy Paw. He was a shapeshifter, alright."

Spoon's head rocks back. He tucks his hand securely in his shirt. Just before he passes out, he tells himself that if she ever comes back, he will marry her. No matter how old or how ugly she turns out to be.

Darkness, darkness, darkness. Darkness can obscure, but it can also comfort. It depends, of course, on how one chooses to accept it. If a phone rings and we answer, how responsible are we for whoever, or whatever, is on the other end?

CHAPTER 64

KATE

Here is what I need to tell you:

First, none of this is happening the way I planned. I thought that I'd have something for you. Something good, at least a real house and a real life. I mean a steady one, where there isn't so much happening, and we have time to think. Your grandmother says that never comes, but if it's so impossible, I'm not sure why anyone keeps trying.

So you should know I won't stop trying. That isn't enough, of course. You'll find out that trying is hardly ever enough. But sometimes you get lucky, and I guess that has to be enough. To hope for, I mean.

I got lucky with your dad. Most people don't think I did, but they don't know Connor like I do. He's trying hard. He truly is. He just hasn't gotten lucky yet. We haven't either, I guess. But who knows? I'll try to believe that you're it. Maybe, in some way, neither of us understands just how lucky you are. And maybe, once we finally get out of here, you'll be the reason this is worth it.

CHAPTER 65

MARCH

The inspector's truck growls its way up the gravel path, tires dragging loose stone into the ditch. March stands on the porch, arms folded, watching the dust bloom behind it. The truck is clean, too clean for the valley, and March already doesn't like him.

The man climbs out and straightens his collar. He's short, with a clipboard and a limp handshake.

"Kyle Fen," he says. "Spoon sent me up."

March nods once. He doesn't shake. He steps aside.

Kyle walks in like he owns the place, his boots too loud on the wood. He taps the walls with his knuckles. Snaps pictures with his phone. Makes sounds like "hmm" and "oof" and "Jesus."

"It's old," March offers, finally.

Kyle grins nervously. "That's one word for it."

They stand in the kitchen. The light above the stove flickers and then steadies, like it's listening.

Kyle leans on the counter. "You know this foundation's slipping, right?"

March nods.

"You get water down here every spring?"

"It's gotten worse since the pump quit."

"Are you planning on fixing it?"

"Planning on it, sure."

Kyle scratches something onto his clipboard. "Look, off the record—this place isn't safe. Not just code-wise. I mean, the damn joists are bowing, and that back porch? I wouldn't lean on it too long."

March shrugs. "Not many people leaning on it."

"You live alone?"

March doesn't answer.

Kyle looks around. "I've seen worse. But not by much. And not where people are still sleeping."

There's a pause. March picks up a mug that Cathleen once painted blue and sets it back down without sipping. "So what's Spoon want?"

Kyle waves it off. "It's not a threat. It's a heads-up. Spoon's got folks looking to build up here—might want this land. He said maybe you'd want to get ahead of things. Sell, relocate. Before it falls in."

"I built this house with my father," March says.

Kyle doesn't flinch. "Yeah, I figured. Sentiment is a hell of a thing. But this place? It's leaning into the hill like it wants to slide."

March nods slowly. He's been feeling it, the way the doors don't shut right anymore. The draft that comes through in the mornings, like a hidden whisper.

Kyle steps to the door. "I'm just doing the paperwork. You want it on file as condemned, I'll write it soft. But if anyone official takes a look, they'll write it loud."

"Thanks," March says.

Kyle eyes him. "You got somewhere else to go?"

March shakes his head.

Kyle hesitates, then heads out. The truck stirs the gravel again and is gone.

March stands in the doorway for a long time, watching the dust settle. He imagines the house cracking down the middle. He imagines it gently folding in on itself, like paper soaked too long.

He closes the door carefully behind him.

Where light flickers, there is doubt.

CHAPTER 66

LORRAINE

Lorraine is somewhat less than pleased with Kate's new home. There's nothing wrong with the house itself except the usual issues, such as broken hinges, leaky pipes, and chipped paint. It is on a small cul-de-sac at the end of a long row of old mining homes, simple two-story blocks with pitched roofs and showers in the cellars. Wooded lots are all that remain of some of them, left vacant and eventually bulldozed (who knows why) when the Federal Mine changed hands. Connor's house (she supposes she should start calling it Kate's) has been renovated, updated, and otherwise tinkered with by its many previous owners so that it now looks like something thrown together from leftover parts.

What troubles her about the house is its lack of order and the absence of evidence supporting any semblance of a comfortable routine. To Lorraine, it looks as though her daughter is living like a drifter.

But mostly, she's thinking of Hem and Trevor alone back at the house. She isn't used to being the one out after dark. To occupy herself, she tries to remember the last time she spent a night away from here. It is a long time—longer than she cares to dwell on. Of course, it isn't much different here than it is in the valley, as long as she keeps her eyes on the window.

The night is dark; no moon to speak of. But the stars are clearer here, or so it seems. They remind her of the winter sky. Her eyes are drawn down suddenly, towards a shadow at the end of the drive. Two shadows—one much taller than the other. They come up the drive as one, then split at the hood of Kate's car. The smaller one disappears, and the other continues around to the trunk.

"Kate!"

She hears a clatter from the bedroom, then silence.

"There's someone out by your car. I think they're trying to get in."

Outside, she can see the child (it must be a child) come around to the back of the car, where he helps to open the trunk.

Finally, Kate's footsteps sound out in the hall, and Lorraine meets her halfway, guiding her quickly towards the window.

"Do you know them?" Lorraine asks.

Kate nods. "It's Fay Sullivan."

CHAPTER 67

KATE

"Fay, what are you doing? Is something wrong? You can't just come here like this."

Fay turns back to the trunk and begins rifling its contents, stuffing things into her pockets. Mason has returned to the edge of the street and is waiting for his mother. In the darkness, he's an almost perfect shadow. He's wearing a sweatshirt, and the only way that she can tell he's real is by a hole in his jeans, through which his pale skin shines.

"Fay—"

"—we won't come back again."

"—you can't break into my car."

Fay snaps around to face her.

"I already got it. It's Spoon's anyway. That makes it mine."

Kate is silent for a moment, noticing the fear in Fay's voice. It is harsh and real—a pure fear without object.

In the pause, Fay seems to make a decision. She slams the trunk shut and, carrying what she took beneath one arm, starts moving quickly down the drive. Kate thinks that this will be the end of it. She's inclined to let it go. But then Fay reaches Mason, who resists her attempts to move him. When she lets him go, he bends down to tie his shoe.

Kate is suddenly uncomfortably aware of Lorraine's shadowy presence, peeking out at them from behind the blinds. She calls out, "What do I tell Connor?"

Mason stands, and Fay immediately gets him walking. Her response appears to echo, disembodied, from the darkness.

"Tell him it's a fucking dream."

CHAPTER 68

LORRAINE

Lorraine doesn't wait for the echo to fade. She opens the door before it finishes swinging, steps barefoot onto the porch and down the steps two at a time. The wind is sharp; her cardigan flares open like a broken sail. By the time she reaches the gravel, Fay and Mason are almost to the road.

"Fay," she calls.

Fay stops but doesn't turn. Mason keeps walking. Lorraine catches up, breath clouding in the dark. She's forgotten her shoes, and the gravel bites up into the arches of her feet, sharp enough to keep her present.

"I heard something," she says. "About the girl at Fitz's. The waitress. Is it true?"

Her voice sounds smaller than she'd meant it to.

Fay's eyes flick open. "What exactly did you hear?"

"That she was hurt. That Spoon—"

"Then you heard enough."

Lorraine folds her arms tight across her chest. The cold is creeping in at the sleeves, slipping down her back. But it's not the cold that makes her shiver.

"I just want to know what's real."

Fay exhales smoke that's been sitting in her lungs too long. "It's real enough."

"Did you see it?"

"I saw what he looked like after. That was enough."

Lorraine feels her stomach coil. Her voice, when it comes, is a whisper that barely clears her throat.

"Well, shit, Fay. You should tell somebody."

"No." She shakes her head vehemently. "It's been too long. I've had *all* my turns. We both have. And also because he still scares me. That means I'd say it like I was asking permission."

Lorraine crosses her arms. "So what, I confront him and what? He apologizes? He changes?"

"No," Fay says. "But you won't have to keep pretending not to know."

Lorraine presses one palm against the other. Her jaw is set tight.

"You aren't scared of him," Fay says. "You're angry. And that means he might actually listen."

"It doesn't matter if he listens."

"It matters that you say it."

They are standing in the dark now, half-lit by the porch lamp Lorraine forgot to turn off. Mason is already gone from view. The wind is picking up again.

"You want me to call the cops?"

"I want you to make a choice," Fay says. "That's more than I ever did."

Lorraine thinks of Trevor, of the boy he is and the man he might become. She pictures his hands building something from scratch, something that flies. She wonders what kind of man he'd be if all he ever saw was silence.

"All right," she says. "But not tonight."

Fay nods. "Tomorrow's good. Tomorrow he'll still be the same man."

CHAPTER 69

BAR

Spoon wakes to the sound of breaking glass and the smell of cinnamon whiskey. Opening his eyes, he sees a pair of work boots kicking through the shattered remnants of a bottle. From a gash in the boot leather, threads of cotton stuffing hang like twisted white worms, trailing bits of mud.

"The fuck you doing?" Spoon says.

He's answered by the clattering of bottles as the boots scramble around the other side of the bar.

Spoon is much too blinded by his scratched-up eyes and throbbing brain to see straight, but he recognizes March's voice when he says, "Good. I thought I'd be here all day." Spoon sits up and feels everything in both his head and chest pitch forward as though it has hardened into one dead mass and torn loose.

There is whiskey dripping from the counter down the back of his neck.

Mentally, he reaches out in search of joints and vertebrae, feeling every muscle, tendon, and digit in its place. This is the first time drugs have failed him—there is no denying that they have, despite how many times he tells himself the beer was warm. Instead of keeping him in balance, they have turned him into something like the rabid brute his father was. He knows he must stay confident and stay strong, now more than ever.

Reaching out for something to hold onto, his hand lands inside a plastic bowl of lemon slices. He lays back down on the floor and sucks them, one after another, as his aching head distracts itself by working on the mystery of the man in the wounded boots. Above him, the wire racks are empty. There is hardly a bottle left. Not even the few jars of wine he keeps for truly hopeless drunks who have acquired a taste for it.

"March," he says. "Say everything's okay."

"It's all right," March says. He's pouring them both tall glasses of gin. "We closed the bar. Made sure everybody understood to keep their mouths shut."

"Good," Spoon says. He takes the glass from March's outstretched hand, drinks, spits it out, and drinks some more. When the final lemon has been sucked dry, he is loath to let it go. He pulls it in between his lips and bites the rind.

March stares down at the counter, playing with the sweat on his glass.

"What is it?" Spoon asks.

They both fall silent, and the sound of buzzing insects fills the room. March finishes his drink before answering.

"I found out this morning—someone called it in."

"Shit. How do you know?"

"I just think it wouldn't be a good time—"

"Who?" Spoon asks. He's breathing heavily.

"Hem. That vet, down in the valley."

Spoon backs up a little, coughs, and spits onto the floor. The room is wavering around him.

"It's a slope," he says and chokes a little on his drink. "You can't let someone get ahead of you. Especially someone like that." He shakes his head. "Ambitious. Smart. A guy like that, you have to keep him down. You have to make him think he's dumb."

March reaches for the bottle.

"You don't have to tell him anything. Just find him, knock him down, and beat him all to shit."

"It's not a good time."

Spoon clears his throat and stares into the middle distance. "You know the things my father used to do?"

"Some. Just like everybody else."

"You don't know anything. Thank god."

March nods. "What I do know makes me glad I didn't know him."

Spoon sighs. "He was a terrifying man."

When March leaves, Spoon lies on the bar top, buffeted by imperceptibly shifting darkness, as the sun climbs over the line of tall trees that edge the delta, as the first gulls argue loudly in the marsh, as black flies take to the air and fight each other for the drops of drying blood on the bar steps; as the mice that have been stepping lightly all night long between the clapboard walls finish up their crumbs and bed down for the day, and as the silvered insects in the tall grass sing the world into quiet. He waits until he feels the air heat up and settle, sweating out the poison from the night before. Then he rises and goes home.

CHAPTER 70

KATE

The orchard smells like rain and fermenting bark. The trees are half in bloom—patches of pink and white like someone forgot to finish painting. Underfoot, the grass squishes, still heavy with runoff. Connor lays the blanket across the tailgate anyway.

Kate hops up beside him, her boots muddy and her knees scraped from earlier, when they climbed the fence behind the abandoned grange hall. She's been laughing since then, and it still hasn't worn off.

"Don't lean too far back," Connor says, "you'll slide straight into the creek."

"There's a creek now?"

"There is if it keeps raining."

They sip from the thermos he brought. Something herbal, something hot. Kate doesn't ask what.

"Road's washed out at Mania," he says. "The bridge is gone."

"So we don't take Denton."

"I thought I'd try the lower ridge. Stay above the flat."

She pulls her knees to her chest, chin resting on them. The truck ticks as it cools.

"What if we stall out?"

"Then we stall out," Connor says. "Push the truck into the creek and take the rest on foot."

Kate smiles. "Romantic."

"I brought waterproof matches."

She bumps his shoulder.

"I'm serious," he says. "We leave tomorrow. I've got half a tank and two hundred bucks."

"And a baby," she says.

He doesn't answer, but the look he gives her is one she remembers from the night he carried her to the house in the rain. She was barefoot then, too.

"I don't want to give birth in a flooded-out shed in Cavalcade," she says.

"You won't."

The orchard's quiet except for the whistle of wet wind and the distant knock of a branch falling somewhere uphill.

"You think they'll notice right away?" she asks.

"No," Connor says. "Not until it gets quiet."

Kate stares past the trees, towards the edge of Shokten, where the ridgeline blurs into mist. She can almost see the curve of the road that will carry them out.

"Okay," she says. "We'll go."

He exhales like he's been holding it. They sit that way a long time, passing the thermos back and forth until it's empty and warm between their palms.

"Five o'clock?" she says.

"I'll honk once."

She nods, then leans into him, her cheek against his shoulder.

The trees drip around them, blooming.

CHAPTER 71

MOUNTAIN

Mason is face-down in bed, stifling a sob, when he hears a distant rasping, which he takes for the forgotten voice of the mountain. He jumps up, running to the window, where he sees a long white trail of smoke. It arches far above the valley—higher than his window, higher than the sun.

"Mason!"

There is dog hair in his nostrils and dust upon the pane. The rocket powers through it, disappearing somewhere out above the sea.

"Mason!"

Spoon's voice sounds like falling stones. It reaches him already in a topple, breaks, and clatters down the steps, where it rebuilds itself and flies back up again.

"Yes, sir."

He hears his father sigh.

"No school today. You stay up in your room, you heard? If there's anything you need, you tell your mother."

Mason nods, and it appears his father hears.

CHAPTER 72

KATE

The house is quiet. Lorraine took Trevor into town for his checkup, and the dog's asleep under the table, paws twitching as if running in a dream. Hem sits by the stove, one knee crossed over the other, his eyes not quite closed. Kate comes in with two mugs of tea and sets one near him without a word.

"Thanks," he says.

She sits across from him. The table's old and marked with the ghosts of meals long gone—burn rings, nicked edges, a faint stain that looks like a bird in flight. She traces it with her finger.

"I'm not coming back," she says.

Hem doesn't answer right away. The kettle ticks on the back burner, cooling.

"I mean," she says, "I'm not sure I can."

He nods once. Sips his tea. It's too hot, but he doesn't flinch.

The wind rattles the loose pane in the window over the sink. Outside, the sky hangs low, bright in that strange way it sometimes gets before a storm. Everything is quiet and too visible.

"I think Connor's a good man," Hem says.

Kate tilts her head. "Since when?"

"Since I stopped pretending I had any say."

She smiles, just slightly.

He goes on. "He listens when you talk. I've seen that. Not many people around here do that with women."

She shrugs. "He's still learning how to say anything back."

"Then you're well-matched."

Kate looks at her father. Really looks. The lines in his face, the calluses along his fingers. She used to think of him as permanent. Now he seems like someone caught mid-sentence.

"I'm scared," she says. "But not of him. Not even of leaving. Just scared I won't become anything."

Hem nods, thoughtful. "No one does. You just keep choosing. That's the trick. You keep choosing, and eventually it starts to look like a life."

She lets that sit, sipping her tea. The dog stirs but doesn't wake.

"I'll write," she says.

"You better."

When she stands to leave, he reaches for her hand, holds it for just a second longer than expected.

"Tell Connor to check the brake lines before the pass. It's been wet lately."

Kate nods. "I will."

She doesn't cry. Neither does he. But when she steps outside, the air feels fuller than before.

CHAPTER 73

VALLEY

The fog has soaked up the porch steps by the time she comes out, her boots making no sound on the boards. Trevor is sitting with his knees drawn up, tracing a line between the railings with the edge of a nail. The dog is quiet behind the door. The lights inside are off.

She sets her bag down beside the door, but doesn't reach for the knob. She doesn't sit, either. Just leans there a while, arms folded under the fringe of her coat, like someone waiting for something she doesn't want to start.

"I should've said goodbye before," she says.

Trevor shrugs. His head is low but he's watching her. Her hair is pulled back like it was the night of the storm. The fog clings to the legs of her jeans.

She says, "I figured it might not be too late."

He nods, but doesn't look at her. The sky above the barn is bright, but not in a way that means anything. It just is.

"I won't be gone long."

He says, "You said that last time."

"I know."

Her boots scuff softly. She moves towards the porch

swing, hesitates, then sits with her hands flat on either side of her. They don't speak for a while. The wood ticks beneath them. In the trees, something flutters, then settles. A single car engine hums, parked somewhere out of view, idling patiently.

She says, "I remember when you used to follow me around with your little tape recorder. You'd make me do fake interviews."

"I remember."

"You used to call me the governor."

"I remember that too."

Kate laughs, just a little, just once. Then she says, "You stopped doing it. I think I was mean about it."

Trevor shrugs. "I didn't really have anything to say."

"You always had more to say than you thought."

There's something in her voice he's never heard before. Not tiredness. Not regret, exactly. Just the sound a person makes when they've stopped trying to explain.

He picks at the splinter in his thumb, presses until the skin goes white. "I'm glad you came out here."

Kate shifts, tucks a strand of hair into her collar. "I wasn't going to."

"I know."

They sit that way until the air turns colder. A breeze pushes in from the creek. She doesn't flinch.

"I don't know if I'm doing the right thing," she says.

Trevor wants to look at her, but doesn't. He stares instead at the knot in the wood below his shoes, where a wasp made its home last spring. "It's still a thing."

She doesn't answer. He wonders if she heard him. Her hand is close now. Not touching. But close enough to feel.

He says, "I used to think if you stayed here long enough, it'd make you like everyone else."

"And now?"

He shrugs. "Now I think the ones who leave... they're just the ones who can still see something else."

She lets out a breath, barely audible. Her hand slips towards his. He doesn't move.

He wants to tell her it's okay not to be brave, but forgets how to say it. So instead he pulls her fingers into his and holds them there, light as thread.

The porch creaks. The fog climbs higher. Her ride pulls up, headlights off.

Kate stands, but doesn't let go. "You'll be okay?"

He nods.

She leans down and kisses the side of his head. Then she's gone.

The swing rocks once behind him, then stops.

Trevor stays on the porch until the mist takes everything, even the tail lights, even the sound of her leaving. When he finally stands, his hand is still warm where hers had been, and he doesn't know what to do with it.

CHAPTER 74

CHURCH

He arrives late this time, shoulders hunched, jacket slung heavy over one arm, his good boots streaked with something red and flaking. The men are already tuned and playing. The first notes of a ballad about an old miner's widow drift out into the lot, where he pauses to finish his drink. He leaves the bottle on the front seat.

Inside the church, it's warm, too warm. Dust sifts through stained-glass windows. He steps in and sees that some of the men have turned to glance—not a full look, just that flicker, that shoulder-hitch that means a name has risen like steam.

He finds his spot up on the balcony. The old pew there has a split in the wood that catches his pant leg when he shifts too hard. He runs his hand down the groove as he sits, remembering how it cracked one winter when the roof leaked and the boards warped in the cold. He thinks about the waitress—how her arms were small, soft. How the edge of the table caught her hip when she tried to push past him. He had meant only to steady her, then only to stop her, then only to teach her, and then—nothing. Only the rhythm of it. Only the pressure that rose in his throat and demanded to be loosed.

Now the pastor plays the harp, slow, somber. A song about loss. Spoon lets the words roll past without catching. He's not sorry—not in the way they want—but he knows what this means. He can see it in the lines of tightened shoulders down below. No one turns. No one smiles. Their heads are bent like wheat before the wind.

He stays for one song, then half of another. When the third begins—an upbeat number, meant to liven things up— he rises. Not fast, not slow. Enough to be noticed, but not remarked on. He straightens his shirt, dusts his thigh with one palm. He doesn't look at the little girl in the aisle who watches him leave.

Outside, the wind has picked up. The air tastes like rain and iron. He lights a cigarette and walks towards his truck.

He thinks briefly about not coming back next week. He thinks about how that would feel—not absence, exactly, but subtraction. A version of himself peeled off and discarded. Then he remembers the music. The way the harp cuts the room. The way the notes always end more softly than they begin.

He flicks ash off his knuckle, watching it scatter on the hood.

The church door creaks shut behind him.

No one follows.

Chapter 75

Ford

As the crow flies, there are no more than a hundred miles between Providence and Shokten. It would be an easy drive if it were not for the imposing mountain range that separates them and that twists the road so ruthlessly that sometimes it breaks down against the strain and scatters into pieces. When this happens, all the pieces tumble down the slope into the streams, which carry them, by almost imperceptible degrees, down to the tip of the peninsula and out into the sea. It's not uncommon for a chunk of yellow asphalt, which has already cut short a number of long-overdue vacations, to be picked up on the beach in Mania by children out in search of shells.

This morning, on the day he promised they would make their escape, Kate wakes her husband before dawn. When she strips the blankets from his body, Connor rolls aggressively away from her and digs his face into his pillow. She can read his naked body like a diary—the yellow bruising down his side from falling on a folding chair, the scratches on his arms from stumbling through bushes, looking for a place to piss; his feet all wrinkled, and his fingernails all broken.

Circling the bed, she finds a sore spot on his shoulder. Purple finger marks left over from a punching contest with a friend. She puts her thumb against it and pretends that it's a knife.

The rain starts falling just as they are setting out. Connor drives with eyes fixed only loosely on the road. He has a cup of coffee balanced on the seat between his knees and grimaces through every sip. They drive until the dirt road turns to gravel and the gravel to pitted asphalt. The drizzle turns into a shower, which, by the time they start to climb the first real hills, has turned into a downpour. Kate has spent all night imagining a perfect sunrise over the peninsula behind them. Now, she turns back and sees nothing in the rearview but a silver, shimmering blockade.

"Maybe we should stop and wait it out," she says.

Connor sighs and shakes his head. "Rain like this won't ever stop."

They drive a few more miles, Connor hunched up like a gargoyle, keeping a steady but imperfect watch above the wheel. They turn a corner, and the rain starts beating from the side instead of from behind. The road begins a steep descent into a narrow hollow. Kate leans forward, peering through the rain-soaked windshield, and her heart sinks. At the bottom of the hill, the road ends in a torrent, at least twenty feet across.

Connor slows the truck down to a crawl, then stops and throws his weight against the brake.

"Do you know a way around it?"

He holds his fingers at his temples, squeezing like a vise. "The logging road, but that's downhill from here. We'll find it worse."

Kate sighs and leans her head against the window, watching as the red-black water washes by. She feels now, more than she has ever felt, a longing to be gone. She feels the power of the boundary between freedom and constraint. She's surprised that she has not begun to cry.

"I'm sorry," Connor says. He tips his head back, drinks his coffee down, and throws the empty cup into the back. "At least no one in Providence knows us. It won't matter if we show up wet."

He has put the truck in gear, and they are moving forward towards the pass.

"You're going through?"

He nods. "We'll make it. Watch your door, though. Water's coming on that side."

Kate leans towards him as they start to ford the stream. The further they go through, the more attentive he becomes. By the time they reach the middle, he seems fully conscious and is muttering a steady stream of colorful encouragements.

The stream isn't as deep as Kate imagined. Still, it rises up above the side rails and, as Connor promised, starts to trickle in beneath her door.

"Don't worry," he says, just before the truck stops moving forward, and they hear its wheels begin to spin.

The carpet underneath her feet is soaked through. Tucking up her feet, she crouches on the seat and stares at Connor, who has opened his door and stands unsteadily upon the runner, staring down into the flood.

"Should I get out?" She asks. "If we're stuck—what about the bags?"

He starts to laugh, and when he turns back, he is smiling. "Don't worry. We won't miss it. Can you get behind the wheel?"

He leans in, kisses her, and says it's only good they started out so early. Then he jumps into the water, wades around the back, and starts to push.

CHAPTER 76

LORRAINE

Lorraine finds him in a shed behind the kennel, the one with the patched roof and the smell of old gasoline and rusted metal. She's never been this close to him before—not really. Seen him at the Lanes, heard his name like a warning—but never this close. He's supposed to be a shadow. A story told when someone needed a reason to lock the back door.

Spoon is hunched over a bench, fiddling with a chain, sleeves rolled, his face turned just enough to see the hollow under his eye. A radio wheezes out some garbled country tune. His movements are slow, like someone killing time, not fixing anything.

She doesn't knock. Just steps in and lets the door shut behind her. It sounds louder than it should.

He doesn't look up. "You lost?"

"No." She takes a slow breath. "I'm Lorraine."

That gets him to raise his eyes. He squints at her like she might be a trick of the light.

"I know who you are," he says. "You're Hem's wife."

"That's true."

He sets the chain down. "So what brings you?"

"I didn't want to come here, but I figured you'd be hiding, so I had to."

It's a gamble—sounding brave when she feels anything but. Her stomach is tight. She didn't even tell Hem where she was going. Didn't want to see the look on his face.

Spoon wipes his hands on a rag, slowly. Like he's stalling. "I'm not hiding. I'm working."

"I want to know why you did it," she says. "The dog. The waitress. Trevor's party. All of it."

He chuckles, but there's no humor in it. "You think I planned any of this?"

"I think you're not the type to lose control."

"Yeah?" He picks up a wrench, turns it over in his hand like it's something alive. "You ever wake up and realize half your life's made up of things you didn't mean?"

Lorraine steps closer. Her hands feel too visible. She curls one into a fist behind her back.

"You *hurt* her," she says.

He doesn't deny it. He just sets the wrench down with a quiet clink. She hates how calm he looks.

"I don't understand you," she says. "You have power. And you use it like a dog pissing on trees."

Spoon looks at her, something sharp flickering in his eyes. "Because that's all it is, Lorraine. All anyone respects. You know how many people have told me to be better? To make it right? And how many of them ever came back when I tried?"

She exhales. Doesn't know what answer she expected. Maybe none. Maybe she just needed to hear the rot spoken aloud.

"So you gave up."

"No," he says. "I got efficient."

There's silence again. The radio warbles through a verse.

Rain starts tapping on the metal roof. It smells like oil and dirt and something old that never fully dried.

"You want to scare people into silence?" she asks. "I think you forgot not everyone's scared of you."

"I don't want anything from you," he says. "So what are you doing here?"

She steps closer, careful not to let her hands shake. She can feel her pulse in her teeth.

"I want you to know I see you. You walk around like everyone owes you something. But what you really want is to be untouchable."

Spoon doesn't move. He doesn't blink. Just watches her, like she is something under glass.

"That's what keeps people in line," he says.

"No," Lorraine says. "That's what makes people leave."

The radio crackles. A thunderhead groans outside. The smell of oil thickens in the air.

"People have been talking about you for years," she says. "You just finally gave them a reason to act."

"You came all the way out here to say that?"

"I came out here so you'd know who called."

She turns, opens the door, and steps out into the rain.

Chapter 77

March

The faucet drips at a rate he has come to trust. It keeps time better than his watch, which he can no longer adjust without setting it backward. He watches the drip fall into the crusted sink and doesn't move. His arm is asleep beneath him. He doesn't lift it.

Outside, the sky is mid-gray. Not the kind that threatens rain, just the kind that seems like it might mean something if you stared at it long enough. The ceiling sags a little, but he tells himself it has always sagged like that. He remembers a line his father used to say—about how houses aren't made to last, they're made to surrender slowly.

His fingers twitch on the table, where an empty cup rocks slightly on the uneven surface. He has been awake since four. Or possibly two. The dog barked, or maybe it was the neighbor's. There are sounds in this house that don't have sources.

Cathleen's coat still hangs on the door. He thought about moving it last week. Or he dreamt he had. Either way, it's there.

He tries to summon a single reason to stand. There's still whiskey in the back cabinet, but the idea of getting it feels like trying to retrieve something that drifted too far into the surf. He imagines the cabinet opened—sees it, even. But that doesn't make it real.

The day presses against the windows like fog on a windshield. Vague shapes come and go—birds, possibly, or bags caught in the wind. He once read somewhere that birds will sometimes spiral downward out of confusion, mistaking fog for open sky. He wonders if people can do that too.

A single beam of light falls across the kitchen floor, lighting the edge of a dead fly and the toe of his boot. He moves his boot. The light remains.

A thought stirs, then turns to ash. He imagines a life where he did things differently—not better, just not the same. One where he fixed the roof when he said he would. One where he never took the call from Spoon. One where Cathleen didn't find out.

The house creaks. He tells himself the wind has shifted.

He places both hands flat on the table and leans forward like a man preparing to rise. But the impulse fades, weakens, passes.

The fly remains. The drip continues.

And March tells himself there's no point rushing the end of anything.

Chapter 78

Spoon

E ven after he has broken every lightbulb in the house (despite his fear that Fay will burn the place down with a candle), even after he has broken every bottle, every jar, and nearly every windowpane, there still isn't enough glass. So Spoon searches through the basement, finding three large boxes full of nails and one containing carpet tacks. He sends his son into the sheds, and Mason digs up safety pins, a few box-cutter blades, and dozens of old fish hooks.

While the sun is setting, Spoon snaps all the blades from kitchen knives and plants them in the dirt. By nightfall, he has made a fence he can be happy with—an apron of sharp objects stretching from one corner of the house to the other, with the front porch at its center.

Feeling suddenly unsure of himself once the fever of this work has passed, Spoon leans against his door and hides his ears behind his hands. He has been breaking glass all afternoon, and now the sound repeats inside his head. It is a horror, gross and inexplicable. No matter how he tries to think about it, it won't end.

There comes a moment when he sees things clearly once

again. A moment when he knows that he can beat this trouble in the same way he has beaten trouble many times before. All he has to do is stay collected and retain the upper hand.

A moment later, he feels sorry—not just for himself, but for everyone at once. He pities everything.

Spoon stumbles through the house into the living room and tumbles down onto the couch. His men will be here in an hour, and his mind is filled with dogs pressed nose-to-tail, all in a panic as they jostle towards the exit. He can't remember feeling sober.

CHAPTER 79

TREVOR

Trevor's leg still hurts him, but he's dealing with it well. He doesn't want to let it show. Even so, tonight is especially hard. He has lain awake, both to monitor the throbbing—which is getting better but still refuses to be ignored—and to try to calm it by thinking about Lily. He has decided that it isn't so much that he wants her, but that he likes her, and is frightened by the way she's grown attached to Mason. He no longer knows his friend; he's unaware of what he's dealing with, but he knows that, nonetheless, there has been some significant change. He's smart enough to know that Mason is slowly becoming like his father.

It is difficult to put this in perspective. He doesn't want to lose the only friend he has. But he has to admit that Mason has become unmanageable. He's selfish now—Trevor sees it in his eyes and in his movements, his postures. If Mason were a dog, Trevor's father would undoubtedly pronounce him rabid.

A sound rises—not the wind, but sharper. Sirens. Not close, not far. Traveling the length of the road out near Mason's, the curve where kids leave flowers now and then, for no reason anyone remembers. He rushes out of bed and down the hallway, where he finds his parents up as well, sitting silently across from one another on the bed.

"That's going to their house, right?"

"Yeah."

"Is he dead?"

Hem exhales through his nose. "I don't know."

Another pause. The sirens fade into the hills, swallowed by distance and the weight of everything they pull behind them.

"Come here," his mother says, and Trevor climbs up on the bed between them. She lays him on his back, his head against a stack of soft, clean pillows. He tries mentally to push against her touch, but it's far too soft. Too smooth. He sinks.

Trevor lies back. "It doesn't seem fair."

Hem waits until Trevor's breathing slows before speaking again. The boy is still awake—he always is—but they both pretend otherwise for a little while. It makes the dark quieter.

Outside, the wind lifts the branch against the gutter. Hem listens. He's been hearing that sound since he was Trevor's age —different house, same wind.

"You remember the Fourth of July," Hem says, low, not really a question. "When you cried 'cause the fireworks were too loud, and Lorraine made you a fort out of lawn chairs and towels."

Trevor doesn't move, but his voice comes flat into the pillow. "You said it was a war outside."

"I didn't mean it literally."

"You said I could pick which side I was on."

Hem smiles. "I still think that's true."

They're quiet again. Trevor sits up slightly, just enough to look. Hem thinks about that. There's a photo somewhere— him and Lorraine on their wedding day, Mason holding the rings, too small to understand. The picture is still in a drawer, he thinks. Or maybe in the garage. Nothing ever really disappears, it just gets misplaced.

"No," Hem says. "It's not fair. But I don't think fair is what life's trying to be."

Trevor pulls the blanket up. "Then what's the point?"

Hem leans forward, elbows on knees. "There isn't one. Not like that. There's no success or failure. Just a bunch of things that happen, one after the other. You do your best with them. That's all."

"Even the bad ones?"

"Especially the bad ones."

The clock clicks to a new minute. The bulb in the hallway hums.

Trevor says, "So we're just... going through it?"

Hem nods, but Trevor can't see. "Yeah."

"That's kind of sad."

Hem leans back, looking at the ceiling. "It's also kind of free."

Trevor turns towards the wall. His breath slows again, but not in the same way.

Hem reaches out and lays his hand gently on Trevor's back, feeling the small, steady rise of it. When he speaks, it's almost too quiet to hear.

"You're not alone in it, though."

"I know."

And Hem believes him.

CHAPTER 80

SPOON

S poon personally answers every knock upon the door and asks each caller to remove their socks and shoes. He tosses these haphazardly into the hallway closet.

In the kitchen, there is crosstalk, coughing, and the smell of feet—a gallon of white whiskey on the table, anchoring a spread of guns and ammunition.

One of them is only nineteen. He's Spoon's first cousin on his father's side and is usually the first to arrive when called. He wears his youth-like armor.

"First pick," Spoon says.

"Doesn't matter."

Spoon hands him a .45 revolver and a box of ammunition. "Keep back by the door and stay down low. Don't shoot unless you have to."

Spoon pours drinks. His stomach feels like it is full of maggots, and his hands are weak. He holds his father's shotgun by the barrel, resting it beside him on the floor.

"You should turn that thing around," his cousin says. "I know a guy who got a load of duck shot in the face."

Through practice, Spoon has made his mind a great deal

more resilient than the average man's. Despite the costs of drinking, he's not blacked out. But he's close, and now his thoughts are little more than sound and light—police in slick black helmets running up the grade—the sound of helicopter engines swinging, stirring up the stars.

Spoon's uncle, calm, respected, nearing sixty, asks if there is anything to eat. He loads a .38 and shoves it down somewhere inside his shirt, then places Mason's little rifle on his lap.

"Refrigerator," Spoon says.

Someone checks and finds a pepperoni, peanut butter, and a jar of pickles.

"Bread?"

"Off somewhere. Take a look."

March and Flint are sitting close together on the far side of the table, whispering to one another. Spoon watches for a while, then says, "You don't have a gun."

The room is full of sound as men make sandwiches and drinks.

March says, "What's with all the glass?"

Spoon says, "So you don't run."

"You sure it isn't best to get a lawyer?"

Spoon is quiet.

Flint says, "This is all for show, right? Cops in Shokten don't want anything to do with us. They wouldn't stick their necks out. Kids, you know? And all we have to do is play with them."

Now, there are headlights in the drive, and in his mind's eye, Spoon is seeing ghosts. Old men in the chapel, picking stained guitars; the waitress, with her red mouth wired shut; a doe, its legs cracked, lying by the roadside; Mason, in the dark behind the kennel, on the school bus, leaving—always leaving —hunting with his father in the first light, moments of concrete awareness. Old men picking, old men picking—in the echoes, the image of Rig Sullivan, with a gasoline can in his hand, crouched beside a dead dog.

"Wait," Spoon says. "Where's Connor?"

No one answers.

"Where's Connor?"

"I don't know," March says.

Spoon puts his hand to his head. "You think he ran?"

"I don't know, but it isn't exactly a good time to find out."

"No," Spoon groans. "I think you know something."

"But he's right."

The men all turn to Cole, who is leaning against the back door, looking glum and earnest.

Spoon sniffs. "About what?"

"As your doctor, I have to tell you that you're very drunk. Or stoned. I'm not sure which."

Spoon glares at him. "All right."

"So, I don't think you can trust yourself to make decisions right now."

"Maybe," Spoon says and nods.

Cole puts his hands up and begins backing off the door. "I know good lawyers, Spoon. I think it's best you give up, spend a couple of nights in jail, and let them help you out."

"The thing I don't know," Spoon says dryly and clears his throat. "The thing I don't know is whether I can't trust myself right now or whether I can't trust you."

"Shit." Cole drops his head and reaches for the door handle, waving his other hand in the air. "You do what you want, Mr. Sullivan. I'm going to make sure a hundred thousand dollars' worth of your speed doesn't end up seized."

Spoon lets him go, still trying to make sense of what Cole's saying.

CHAPTER 81

COPS

The old sedans ascend the mountain in a row, struggling against the grade. They are not equipped for this road, with its deep ruts, wild curves, and tire-sucking washouts. Shocks hiss, engines grumble—awful sounds in all this dark and silence.

There are three cars carrying four officers along with the Shokten County Sheriff. The sheriff is from Providence and would have stayed there all his life if he had been born to a better family—one with just a little money or prestige. He might have stayed there if he had been born a little smarter or a little more ambitious. But he was born to a poor single father and with only average intelligence and no special ability of any kind. By chance, he has become what he was always meant to be—a mediocre, mildly corrupt administrator in a town far off the beaten path.

One of the officers is a woman who, considering her intelligence and character, is better suited to detective work than street patrols and grade school presentations. But she's only thirty-one years old, and though her family is respectable, it's only by the county's standards, meaning that her relatives have rarely ended up in prison, and her brother, who is currently driving the car ahead of hers, is close to making deputy.

The sheriff and the female officer are looking forward to arresting Spoon. They see him as a menace and believe that his imprisonment will turn the tide of poverty and violence that has swamped the whole peninsula. Her brother, on the other hand, has serious misgivings. He's saying to the man beside him, "Spoon has got to know we didn't have a choice."

"You hope. You know he won't be locked up long."

"Jesus, sometimes I think that waitress had it coming."

"That's 'cause you were drunk. You didn't see him do it."

"Well, she's fine now."

"Mostly. Anyway, we're fucked."

Their headlights shine upon a gray fox crossing the road, and the driver taps the brakes. "We might be fine," he says. "Just once he's taken, we should push to get him moved to Providence."

The other man nods. "Sure thing. No friends there."

He turns to face the window, looking through the darkness towards the valley, where there is a cabin where he lives with his two uncles, who are too unhealthy and slow-minded to live by themselves. Tonight, when he gets home, he has to finish up an essay for a night class he is taking. One day, he will be a man of means, and everything will be all right.

It's not true—he only fools himself—and yet his heart is generally good, unlike the final officer, who is deep inside Spoon's pocket and has been there for much longer than he has been old enough to know it.

Mason hears the sirens and sees the line of cars arriving in the drive. He isn't frightened, only curious to see just what his dad will do. He cracks the window screen and kneels on his bed. Outside, he can see his father and a group of other men standing in a loose formation. Every one of them is stock-still, each holding a gun.

He doesn't think but rushes to his mother's room. He knows enough to know that this is something he is far too young to handle.

"Mom!" he cries out, slamming the bedroom door shut. "Mom!"

Fay is lying on an orange coverlet, the color, Mason thinks, of vomit. She's naked from the waist down, but he doesn't have the time to think about her nakedness—especially the tuft of reddish hair between her legs.

He starts to shake her, crying out for help and an explanation.

Fay doesn't wake up. Her lips are turning blue.

Outside—moonlight, stars, and four policemen standing shocked inside the tender beams of headlights.

Guns are drawn and cocked and lifted everywhere in one aggressive movement. The police back up and hide behind their cars. Spoon's nephew cries out as he steps on a stray glass.

Spoon discovers he is wild. He has lost himself. He turns his back on the police and tells his men to kill them. Wild and inconsolable, he waits to hear the sound. But there is only wind and murmuring—the quiet loneliness of memory—the lonely company of ghosts.

Spoon's uncle coughs. The police chief whispers to his officers, then steps out from behind his car.

"Spoon," the chief says, "Things aren't like they used to be. You can't hurt people just because you're angry."

Spoon is thinking, Pharaoh hound—that bitch. Cole— that bastard. Cole—that speck—he had no right to trick him.

He reaches out and finds March right beside him. They communicate through touches—pressure, and caress—and though he's confused, March finally kneels down.

Spoon is thinking nothing. He has lost himself again. And

now the night is very still, except for insects and the fireflies. And everyone is listening and knowing that a man can never know, and never know, and never know.

Spoon holds the barrel of his father's shotgun up to March's head and pulls the trigger.

CHAPTER 82

VALLEY

Kate's room still looks full. Lorraine knows the dresser is empty, as is the closet. She knows there are no more notebooks stashed beneath the bed or dirty laundry in the crawlspace. But the posters of her favorite bands have stayed, discarded like the glittery horses and beautiful vampires that came before them.

Hem is sitting on her bed examining his nails. He looks like the stress of the past few months has put him past his limit, which has never been particularly high to begin with. He's emotional about the smallest things.

"You okay?"

"Yeah. I'm trying to figure it out. She's barely eighteen."

The room doesn't even smell stale.

She says, "You know."

"No, I really don't. Later, maybe..."

"Maybe?"

"Definitely, then. But later."

"Hem, she just got tired of it. You know how much we hate it here."

His head snaps up. "Not Trevor."

"No, not Trevor. But I feel like we're drifting apart."

His hair is short now. Almost all gray. But she remembers when it was long. He stretches out his arms, and she comes in to meet them. His head is soft between her hands.

"It's my fault."

"No, it's not."

She knows this to be true.

CHAPTER 83

FAY

The alcove hums. A light above the vending machine blinks without rhythm, casting shifting shapes against the tile. Mason is there, hood up, flipping a pencil across his knuckles like it means something.

Fay sees him before he sees her. She pauses near the water fountain, weighing the long way around, then sits across from him without sound, like she'd meant to all along.

He doesn't startle. Just shifts slightly, letting the pencil drop into his lap.

"You get what you wanted?" she asks, her voice too even.

He shrugs. "Wasn't sure what I wanted."

She nods once. "That's honest."

His eyes follow the grout lines on the floor. She's used to that. Boys stare too long or not at all. Mason hovers somewhere in between, as though the space between gazes is the only safe place left.

"You're not a bad kid," she says.

"I didn't ask."

"I know."

This time, he looks at her. His eyes are clearer than she remembers—less glassy. "Why are you always mad at me?"

She doesn't answer. The pencil rolls to a stop between them. She picks it up and doesn't hand it back.

"I'm not mad," she says. "I just don't know what to do with you."

"That's not my fault."

"No," she says. "It's mine."

The light above them twitches. The vending machine hums louder, like it's dreaming.

"When I was your age," she says, "I thought the worst thing in the world was being forgotten."

He doesn't answer.

"I was wrong."

He shifts again, ankle against the leg of the chair. A dull metal clank.

"What is?" he says.

"Being remembered the wrong way."

The pencil rolls off her thigh and hits the floor.

"I never asked you for anything," he says.

"That's the only reason I've stayed this long."

She regrets it the second it's said. As she watches his shoulders fold inward, like something small inside him got hit.

"That came out wrong," she adds.

He shrugs, a softer version now. One that says: it's okay, but not really.

"I don't hate you," she says. "I just don't know how to keep you safe. And that makes me mean."

He nods.

They don't look at each other for a while. The lights above shift tone again, pulling the blue out of the air. A janitor passes. Doesn't stop.

"Are you hungry?" she asks.

He glances at the machine. "Always."

She pulls change from her coat, places it in his hand without touching him. "Don't get the jerky. It's fake."

He stands like the floor might give. "Thanks."

She watches him go. He walks like someone used to being corrected. Careful, but not quiet. This isn't love, she thinks. But maybe it's the beginning of something that could outlast it.

She stays where she is, listening to the low whir of coils turning behind glass, wondering whether or not mercy, begun late, still counts.

CHAPTER 84

MOUNTAIN

Mason waits at the edge of the gravel turnout, where the trees fall away like pulled teeth and the road bends, unsignaled, towards town. The leash hangs slack from his hand, trailing dust, wrapping once around his wrist—not for security, exactly, just because letting go feels like a decision he isn't ready to make.

It isn't yet light. The sky above the hills has begun to pale, but without color. Fog presses in like breath on glass. The woods, the fence line, the cut path down to the kennel—gone. Only the shape of them lingers, stitched into the air.

He listens. Not for anything in particular, just for the small sound that might mean something has changed—a bark, maybe, claws on pavement, the single clink of a collar against gravel. But there is nothing. Only the sizzle of power lines above the trees, and somewhere far away, the dry cough of an engine that won't turn over.

In his pocket, the starling rustles. He feels its claws pricking through the thin lining of his jacket. Its body is warm. It doesn't struggle. Just presses close, like it believes in him.

The bus comes late, just one headlight cutting through the fog. Mason stands slow, knees tight, and waits for the door to stutter open. The driver doesn't look at him. He doesn't expect her to.

He climbs in, the leash looped now and gathered in his fist. He moves to the back, past the empty benches, past the stale smell of sweat and vinyl, and drops into the last seat. Outside, the road unspools beneath them, and behind them, the turnout folds back into mist.

He doesn't look back at the house. Not really. But he sees the pieces of it vanish—mailbox, fence, the crooked post where Spoon used to tie his guards. By the time they reach the bridge, it's all water. A slow, colorless river, swallowing the banks.

He leans his head to the glass. The window hisses against his skin.

He isn't tired. He is something quieter than that.

The starling shifts. He feels it breathing. It doesn't try to escape. He likes that about it.

He thinks of his mother in the kitchen, forehead pressed to the tap, watching the water run because it's the only thing that doesn't change. She said once that he was too still for a child. That she sometimes thought he was sleepwalking.

He thinks of his father's voice outside the kennel, asking how long it takes for dogs to forget who they're angry at. Not waiting for an answer.

He thinks of Trevor—his dumb rockets, his way of pretending not to be scared until it matters.

He lets the leash fall. It slips from his knee and curls on the floor like something lost, not dropped.

He doesn't pick it up.

CHAPTER 85

PROVIDENCE

In the mornings, Kate walks with the stroller along the tree-lined edge of Freedom Park, keeping to the side streets where the sidewalks aren't buckled. The air smells of fresh-cut grass and bus fumes. By the time she reaches the stone arch near the duck pond, the baby is usually asleep, one sock curled beneath his foot like a feather.

Connor is already at the job site—up before sunrise, out the door before she finishes her first cup of coffee. His boots leave a trail of dust on the tile. Sometimes she finds little half-crescents of dried mud where he sat to tie them. He never notices. He moves through the apartment like he's still outdoors.

At the vet's office, she checks vitals, files records, and steadies skittish retrievers. The head doctor lets her sit in on surgeries. Some days, they don't speak much. Other days, he shows her how to press the skin above a cat's eye and feel for heat. Some days she feels like a bone or ligament that had slipped its place, and was now exactly back where it belongs. Other days, she feels like the ligament that had been in place was now knocked astray. She figures that's how healing goes.

They named their son Cole. He doesn't cry much. He blinks with the solemnity of a priest.

On Saturdays, Connor brings back bruised fruit from a vendor he likes—always mangoes, though neither of them asked for them. He chops them messily over the sink and eats with the knife still in hand. "Got a deal," he always says, mouth full, "three bucks for all this."

She smiles and lets it pass.

In the evenings, they eat late. She stands at the stove while Connor holds Cole on his lap, bouncing him gently, humming half-tunes. The boy's eyes follow the fan blades overhead. Sometimes she hums with him. Sometimes not.

One night, after the dishes are done and the baby has gone quiet, Kate stands by the window and watches the tail lights slip past, red beads drawn out in long threads. Across the street, a woman waters her balcony plants with a chipped blue pitcher. The woman wears headphones. She dances.

Connor comes up behind her and places a hand on her shoulder. His palm is warm. She leans into it.

He says, "You thinking again?"

She nods.

"About home?"

She doesn't answer right away.

He says, "It was never really home. Not for you."

"No," she says. "But it was something."

He rests his chin on her shoulder. "Something's not bad."

They stay like that until Cole shifts in the crib and lets out a soft sound—half yawn, half protest.

Connor turns to go. She stays by the window a moment longer. She thinks of fireflies. Of the creek at night. Of Trevor's rockets and the valley's strange hush when all the lights went out.

Now the streets glimmer. Headlights sweep across her feet. She closes the curtain slowly, careful not to wake the baby.

Chapter 86

George

George Eubanks sits shirtless on the edge of the paper-lined exam table, one sock on, one sock off, nursing the tail end of a hangover with the composure of a man used to worse. The window is cracked. The light is too honest.

Doctor Cole enters like he always does—with the air of someone who's already lost the argument but will repeat it anyway.

"Morning, George."

"I'll be the judge of that," George says, and grins.

Cole doesn't look up. He ticks something off on a chart. "You weigh more than last time."

"Muscle."

"It's not."

George gestures towards his stomach. "That's core strength. Hiding in plain sight."

Cole snorts once, then pulls on gloves. He listens to George's chest, knocks twice on his back like checking a melon, and then steps back with the look of someone deciding how honest to be.

"You're a mess," he says.

"But a stable one."

"Your liver enzymes are... not as bad as they should be."

George raises both brows. "I beg your pardon."

"Which is to say, your bloodwork is holding together better than I'd expect."

"Ah. So I'm a medical anomaly."

"You're lucky."

George chuckles. It builds slowly, chest to throat, until he's coughing into his fist. "Christ. You hear that? Lucky. That's beautiful."

Cole starts peeling off the gloves. "It's not a compliment."

"Still counts."

The doctor folds the chart closed. "Cut back, George. You know this. You're not bulletproof."

"But I'm resistant. That's worth something."

Cole leans against the counter. "You ever think maybe you've used up all the resistance?"

George considers. "I think maybe the world's just too stubborn to get rid of me."

The clock ticks loudly. Someone laughs out in the hallway —sharp, unfiltered, human.

Cole says, "Come back in six months. Unless something starts falling off."

George reaches for his shirt. "If it does, I'll send it by courier."

At the door, Cole hesitates. "I mean it. Cut back."

George raises a hand. "You have my attention."

"That's not the same."

"No," George says. "It isn't."

They nod at each other like old war buddies who never served.

Outside, the light has mellowed. George puts on his sunglasses before he gets to the car. He sits there for a moment, engine off, watching people come and go. Young people. Thin ones. Some of them are trying. Some pretending.

He laughs again—quiet this time.

Not as bad as it should be.

He considers this proof that the world has no moral order. And somehow, that comforts him more than anything else.

He drives home quickly, as though any delay might change the shape of things. As though the road, with its familiar dips and slants, might take him somewhere else this time.

The gate clicks open like it always does. The driveway curves soft and smug beneath him. The house is too quiet, the way big houses always are once people stop pretending to fill them. In the study—his study—he pours half a glass of something middling and stands with it, unbuttoned, looking at the books he's read and the ones he never will. Then he pulls the journal down from behind the cookbooks. He blows the nonexistent dust from its edge, just for effect.

He writes without warming up:

Life isn't about failing and succeeding. Life just is. Then, at some point, it isn't*. There isn't much more to say about it than that.*

When he finishes, he leans back, satisfied. He underlines "is" and "isn't" twice. Then he simply sits a moment, watching the light creep across the rug. The drink warms his chest. His fingers ache slightly, but he doesn't mind it. Finally, he closes the journal with a smart flick, like someone putting out a flame. He restores it to its place—precise, familiar–and taps the spine once with two fingers.

"There," he says aloud, to no one. "That one's for posterity."

The room doesn't answer. It never does. He likes that about it.

Chapter 87

Shokten

The dog wakes to the sound of rattling chains. The others are all standing up and yapping, hoping they'll be fed.

The boy comes in, the same boy, but smelling different.

The door stays open.

The boy says, "Sit."

He sits. He knows now.

The boy keeps walking towards the end of the row. He's saying "sit," and "stay," and "quiet." Then he comes back, and the dog can hear the latches falling open. The boy doesn't stop when he reaches him but walks by quickly, springing the cage door open.

The dog looks at the white light coming through the kennel door. He stays still, worried. He has learned his lesson.

Then, the boy goes out and disappears. The dog can smell him on the right side of the door. There is the sound of insects and of panting. In the cages, everyone is waiting.

Then the boy says, "Okay," "Okay."

He's the first one out. The first one running through the

dry grass, the first one following the little lights that lead him towards the woods. Behind him, he can hear the others coming fast: their thumping paws, their yips and wails. He's looking forward. This will be a good night.

Acknowledgments

Early drafts of chapters from this book appeared in *Gulf Stream* (2012), *Redivider* (2016) and *Switchback (2018).*

Author's Notes

In the safety of fiction, there are lessons to be learned from considering dark themes. In life, these lessons aren't worth the experience.

Suicide Prevention Crisis Hotline: 988

Substance Abuse and Addiction Hotline: 1-844-289-0879

As a hunter and gun owner, I appreciate firearms as tools to be used sparingly. As an American, I believe guns *are the problem*. If you agree, please consider donating to Brady United, Sandy Hook Promise, GIFFORDS, or any other of the dedicated organizations working to end the madness.

ABOUT THE AUTHOR

Ryan Burden is a middle school teacher, a doctor of English and Creative Writing, and a graduate of the Warren Wilson MFA Program for Writers. His short story "Coming of Age" won *Redivider's* 2016 Beacon Street Prize for fiction. His novel *Orphans* was shortlisted for the 2024 Steel Toe Books Prose Award. Other work has appeared in *Switchback, Gulf Stream, and JMWW,* among others. He lives in Boston, MA.

———

At Silent Clamor Press, we seek to illuminate the human experience with excitement, elegance, and unflinching honesty. If this work has resonated with you—offering a profound journey or a new way of seeing the world—consider sharing your reflections with others. Your voice enriches the ongoing conversation that keeps literature vital and transformative.

———